The Nine Lives *of* Summer

JEM VANSTON

Published by Two Fat Cats Publishing

ISBN: 978-1-3999-4432-8

Front Cover:

Head of a Calico Cat with Closed Eyes (1819)

by Belgian artist Jean-Bernard Duvivier (1762-1837).

Original in The Rijksmuseum (Image: Public Domain)

About the Author

Jem Vanston (who also publishes as PJ Vanston) was born and brought up in Dartford, Kent.

He now lives in Swansea with his two rescue cats, Honey and Bumble.

The Nine Lives of Summer was written for both children and adult readers, and particularly cat lovers, though the story's message is universal. It is his tenth published book.

Author website: www.vanston.co.uk

Twitter: @9LivesofSummer

Email enquiries:
acatcalleddog@hotmail.co.uk

By the Same Author

Fiction:

Cat Books:

A Cat Called Dog (2013)
A Cat Called Dog (illustrated, child-friendly version, 2015)
A Cat Called Dog 2 – The One with the Kittens (illustrated, 2017)

Satirical Novels:

Crump (2010)
Rasmus – a Television Tale (2016)
Somewhere in Europe: Crump 2 (2020)

Poetry:

Santa Goes on Strike (illustrated, 2018)
The Loved Ones – A Collection of Pandemic Poems about Love and Loss (2022)

Non-Fiction:

Thinking Time: 365 inspiring, amusing and thought-provoking quotes to get you through the year (2021)

CHAPTER ONE

The sky explodes like a firework.

BANG!

I try to hide inside the garden, beside a side-wall, hidden by bushes.

I hope no-one has seen me and that I am safe.

My pointy ears twitch nervously at all the loud sounds around me. I curl up small into a ball with my tail over my face.

Another explosion.

BOOM!

Closer this time. Too close. The noise hurts my ears.

It's even louder than the bin lorries that always frighten me every week.

Even louder than fireworks, or thunder in a storm.

Even louder than a lion's roar or the loudest miaow in the world!

I can smell fire in the air. Burning. Not cooking smell or food burning, so I know there is nothing I can eat.

No, something metal and chemical - an unpleasant smell.

My nose twitches under my paws, and I feel myself shaking a little. I do not like fire or smoke. It frightens me, and all of my cat species.

I close my eyes and pretend to sleep - but I cannot close my ears to the noise.

BANG BANG BANG! go the explosions.

BOOM BOOM BOOM BOOM!

They shake the world like the worst earthquake ever, and it happens every day.

I wish the war would go away.

I wish things could be back to how they were, before the bad people came, before

this all started – the noise and the screaming, the nasty smells and the fear.

My name is Summer, and this is my story.

***

It is Sami who finds me later, hiding in the corner of the garden, after all the firework banger noise has stopped.

"I love you Summer," she says. "I love you *so* much!"

She picks me up and gives me a great big hug. I am purring now. I head-bonk her frightened-looking face and she smiles with her big wide eyes.

It is Sami who named me Summer when I arrived here as a little kitten, so many moons ago now.

She loves my beautiful ginger and white fur coat, my little white paws and chest, and my twitchy tickly whiskers – and tells me so all the time.

She loves it when I twist my tail into a 'question mark' shape.

She loves it when I twitch one ear, then the other.

She loves it when I cross and uncross my paws too.

Sami is a pretty young two-legs kitten. She is ten years old and loves me very much, as I love her. It is my duty as a cat to care for her, always. And I shall. No matter what.

"Three, summer, three!" whispers Sami, holding up three fingers.

So I say:

"Miaow! Miaow! Miaow!"

"Clever girl!" says Sami.

It's always nice when members of the inferior human species state the facts, I find. I purr my approval loudly.

Sami grins and hugs me tight.

Then she holds up four fingers, so I say:

"Miaow! Miaow! Miaow! Miaow!"

Sami giggles with delight.

"You must be the cleverest cat in the whole wide world, Summer," she says, "and the only cat in the world that can count!"

This is wrong of course, but you can't blame humans for not knowing.

I have known many of my species who can count – not all, but a fair few, and many of my neighbours in the streets of this town

too. It's just that we cats do not show off that skill to others.

But I can assure you any cat *knows* when it has caught just *one* mouse and knows that catching three is three times better!

Then Shaheen appears. He is Sami's brother, and is a younger two-legs, seven years old – and a male.

Shaheen is always smiling and laughing, running around wearing his red T-shirt and his bright red coat flapping behind him like a cape. He is always playing at being a superhero – like Superman, Sami says, flying through the air, happy and free.

I like Shaheen, but not when he pulls my tail! Lots of very small two-legs kittens are like that – they get gentler as they get older, I know.

But Sami was never rough, even when she was little, and never pulled my tail either. Well, not hard, anyway.

We go inside. Sami's mum, Miriam, is making dinner and it smells delicious.

She is a very pretty woman with long black hair and big green eyes which always look a bit sad even when she's happy.

Sami's eyes are the same.

My eyes are green too – a different green though.

A cats' eye green.

Her dad, Yousuf, is sitting in his chair, staring into space, frowning. He keeps shaking his head, rubbing his chin and tutting. He hasn't been the same since the war started, since the firework banger sounds began.

I know this means he is thinking, and worried, and that it is best not to disturb him when he is like this.

So I go and sit on a cushion on the highest chair in the room, and wash my paws, all whilst enjoying the cooking smells coming from the kitchen.

I know I shall enjoy some of the food the family is eating.

I always do!

CHAPTER TWO

"Miriam, this is our home – we cannot just leave," Sami's dad says at the dinner table.

I am eating some chopped up meatball from a saucer on the floor. It's delicious, as always. But I do not want any of the salad Sami's mum has made.

Yeuck!

That sort of rabbit food is only fit for humans! And rabbits.

We cats like meat, mostly – and fish, of course. Chicken is my favourite!

"Yousuf, we must go," says Miriam. "There is nothing here in Syria but war and... more war..."

"More war more war!" sings Shaheen through a mouth of meatball.

"No talking with your mouth full!" orders his dad, and then turns to his wife. "We have our jobs, our careers, and the children have schools, friends, lives..."

"But what if we are bombed? What if they come here? They are bad men!"

"They're as bad as each other, both sides."

"At least we'll be alive if we leave," said Miriam.

"And homeless, wandering, illegal refugees, paying those...criminal traffickers to get us out. *They* are bad people, Miriam."

Sami says nothing, but she looks worried.

The firework banger noises have been getting louder lately and have happened more often.

Some buildings not all that far away have been destroyed and lie in ruins. I have explored them when out on my daily patrols. Some cats hunt in the rubble.

Sometimes, big roaring metal monster birds which Sami calls 'planes' fly overhead – they are so loud and make me run and hide. When it first happened, it took Sami ages to find me, I hid myself away so well.

"But..." said Sami, quietly, not wanting to interrupt her parents, "but, dad, please – the bombs, the fighting, it gets closer every day..."

"We're frightened, Yousuf. It's time to leave."

Yousuf looks at Miriam. He sighs, smiles sadly and says:

"As usual, you are right, my love."

"We could go to Turkey, then..." says Miriam.

"No!"

"Others have – many people from the..."

"No!" interrupts her husband again. "We are not criminals, but..."

"But?"

"But... I shall apply for a visa to leave, to the British embassy – it is not in Syria any more, but there are various channels, contacts, the UN, in Turkey... I can do it from the university."

"We are lucky – we are qualified, educated – we can get out. Many can't. We must leave...our beautiful home," says Miriam, and she looks around the room, sadly.

Yousuf is a professor in the university English department, Sami has told me. Miriam teaches there too. They met when students, studying English, which is why they speak the language at home much of the time too.

"Our beautiful home," echoes Yousuf, shaking his head slowly and sighing.

"Thank you, Yousuf," says Miriam.

"Thanks, dad," said Sami. "Thanks, mum – but what will happen to Summer?"

My ears prick up at the name.

"Miaow?" I ask, but nobody answers, or says anything.

Sami looks sad and worried.

"Thank you thank you thank you!" says Shaheen, before jumping down from the table. He grabs his red coat from the hook by the door and runs around with it flapping behind him like a cape, playing superheroes again.

His dad usually tells him off for getting down from the table without asking – makes him get back on his chair and ask politely.

He doesn't this time, though I see him open his mouth slightly as if he is going too – just like when I do a 'silent miaow' to get sympathy so the two-legs will feel sorry for me and give me more treats! But I don't think Yousuf wants treats.

"So many memories," whispers Yousuf, before closing his eyes and bowing his head.

"We still have each other," says Miriam, touching his arm tenderly. "We will always be a family, together."

"Together," says Sami, nodding at her mum, and reaching out to hold each other's hands.

"Everything will be OK," says her mum.

"I know," says Sami.

And I miaow in agreement too.

"Remember how it used to be?" says Sami's dad to her, and she nods as she remembers.

So does Miriam, and also Shaheen when he runs into the living room again.

"Remember the past, when you were little? Before the war?"

"Before the war before the war before the war," says Shaheen.

And they all think back and remember...

The garden is always beautiful in the sunshine, with roses and other colourful flowers blooming everywhere, and a lovely perfumed scent always in the air.

Sami and Shaheen used to love playing all day long in the garden at weekends and in the school holidays. Often, we would all eat outside in the summer evenings on a table brought out from the kitchen, and in the spring and autumn too if it was warm enough.

Sometimes, their school friends were there and Miriam would bring out oranges and cold drinks – and treats for me too!

And I had some cat friends too, who would visit from time to time or pass on the street outside, and other cats I knew, but was wary of as they were bigger than me, and male. They knew not to invade my garden though.

Some of the tomcats were very big and aggressive, and sometimes they'd fight and make an awful caterwauling racket which you could hear all through the neighbourhood some nights. They'd be spitting and hissing and yowling and growling and generally behaving like the most unruly kerfuffle of kittens!

But I would always know it was all just for show – cats very rarely really hurt each other. It happens sometimes, a few scratches here and there, especially with the big toms fighting each other over territory – but not much. We cats are very good at avoiding each other and keeping the peace. Better than two-legs anyway, it seems, what with the human fight happening here at the moment.

The weather always seemed to be sunny every day back then, and everyone was happy all the time – or that is how I remember it.

The children would walk to school through streets that were safe – there were no explosions or air raids or firework banger bombs. There was no war.

Life was good.

Nobody had any idea those days would end, how our old lives would just be swept away by it all.

But end they did, and so suddenly, before we knew what was happening

The good became bad, and then the bad became worse.

And all because of the war that started when the bad people came.

CHAPTER THREE

Weeks went by, and the war got worse.

And still, we were living in the same house in the same town in Syria, with the same firework bangs and bombs exploding almost every day.

Sam's mum did not cook meatballs any more, because there wasn't any meat in the shops, she said, 'and not a lot of anything else'. Hardly any vegetables or fruit either – though we cats don't touch them!

So at home we usually had soup and bread mostly, or pasta, or rice, which I enjoyed eating with some meaty broth Miriam made by boiling up bones.

Sami and Shaheen no longer went to school, and their parents did not go to work either. In the past, I was usually home alone all day long – I often slept through it. Not any more. The house was now full of family life, from morning to night.

In fact, sometimes it was so noisy and I had to go and find some peace and quiet in one of the sleep-rooms – what Sami calls 'bedrooms'.

When the children had lessons at home, taught by their parents, I was there helping when I could. Or, at least giving encouragement and comfort!

Yousuf went into the university from time to time though. He said the phones sometimes work there.

"I have to check on the application, Miriam," he always said. "I can do nothing here with the phones cut off."

"Be careful," his wife would plead.

"I will be fine," he'd say, "and I shall try to buy some food."

"If there is any in the shops," Miriam would then sigh.

"I know it's hard, my love," her husband would say, "but it won't be forever – life will get better, I promise."

"Power cuts, phones dead, water gets turned off at any time – nothing works any more..."

"Our application to leave for the UK is being considered by the Syrian Refugee Resettlement program. We just have to be patient," Sami's dad would always say.

"Patient? But for how long!

"To leave Syria now would set a bad example to the children. To run away and selfishly save ourselves, when so many have to stay. Be brave, Miriam."

"But Yousuf, the bombs and airstrikes get closer every day..."

Then Sami would hug her mum and they would cry. I also know Sami misses many of her friends who have already left the town, escaped from the war.

I tell you what – it's a good job I am here to cheer them all up or I don't know what they would do! We cats are good at that.

Shaheen never gets sad, though – he just keeps running around playing superheroes with his red coat cape flapping behind him and his arms stretched out in from of him like Superman as he flies around the house and garden, and the street outside, past the cast iron gates.

"Don't go too far!" his mum and dad always call after him.

He loves running up and down the road outside, which had more space than the garden, and a long straight pavement to race along.

The streets look very different now from the way they used to.

When I go out on my rounds, I can see for myself how the world has changed.

Much of the town now lies in ruins. The streets and pavements are usually empty – just a few people occasionally scampering around like mice, or maybe rats, trying to find a shop open somewhere that still sells food, no doubt. People, like cats, have to eat.

There are very few wheel-boxes – what Sami calls 'cars' – driving about these days: everyone seems to be staying at home, and many people have gone already. I don't know where they have gone. But they have gone, and some left their pets behind – cats and dogs.

One advantage of so little traffic is that now we can hear the tweety birds sing way more than we used to. I watch them too, up on the telephone lines and flying around twittering.

I go *NYAT-NYAT-NYAT* when I see them.

I cannot help it – this is my cat instinct.

I see stray dogs sniffing around too, sometimes in packs. I am wary of them and *very* careful if they are nearby. They always look so hungry.

They hunt in the rubble, as do the cats who have no *furever* homes. They rip through any litter bins for any scraps of food they can find.

Sometimes, I see a dog with a rat in its mouth. There are more rats now. They are too big for me to catch, and some are very fat. I don't know what they are eating.

Now, fewer wheel-boxes whizzing by would usually be a good thing for us cats, as they create awful pollution smoke and smells, and can be very dangerous for animals. We have all known friends and acquaintances who have been knocked over by cars – wheel-boxes – and the bigger ones – lorries. Some cats survive; some do not, and go 'over the rainbow bridge'. I miss them all.

But life goes on, and it is the duty of a cat like me to be there for the family I have adopted and vowed to take care of.

In return, the two-legs give me as much food as they can spare – which is a lot less than it used to be, to be honest, and I hardly ever get treats any more. However, I do not complain. I know the family is eating less too.

We are all always hungry – myself included.

But, having the good fortune to be born a cat, I am able to supplement my protein intake by catching an occasional mouse, and more than a few spiders, beetles, flies and other insects. Every little helps me keep my strength up!

Sami is always there stroking and hugging me, of course, and I am always there to care for her.

CHAPTER FOUR

As a cat, I have certain duties – a routine to follow.

This reflects the perfect triangle of cat life, our holy trinity, with its three perfect feline priorities: eating, sleeping and washing.

Eating is priority number one, of course. We cats always enjoy our food and think about it much of the time. We also see food in our dreams, and often chase it, in mouse or bird form. If you have ever seen our little paws and whiskers twitch while we are sleeping – well, then we are in the middle of a dream hunt!

Now, needless to say, after eating we cats need to sleep – at least sixteen hours a day. More, sometimes, and when we are older. Not all at once, of course. But in blocks of five hours or so. This allows plenty of time for eating, which I have already mentioned, and relieving ourselves neatly, as is our cat way.

A clean cat is a happy and healthy cat!

Then there's our patrols, which we must do twice a day in order to monitor the local territory and the neighbourhood cat community. It is important that order is kept and that I, as a cat, know everything that is going on, however small and apparently insignificant. Attention to detail is a real cat strength.

For example, I know that some of the cats passing through my territory have no families or *furever* homes, yet are not quite strays. They live in a cat shelter run by a very kind and gentle two-legs man who feeds abandoned and lost cats for free. Some cats just pop in for food too, or an occasional snack, even though they may have homes. An extra meal here or there is always welcome. Many others stay at the shelter permanently. I make it my business to know them all, at least the ones who go out on patrol.

I am wary of the bigger tomcats, of course, and admit to running and hiding from a couple of very rough-looking specimens. Self-preservation is an old cat habit – and a good thing too.

And, of course, we cats are wary of any passing humans, whether in or out of wheel-boxes. They are the most dangerous animal of all.

The third priority is washing, which is why our furry coats are always so well-groomed, beautiful and soft. We cats spend at least three hours a day on this, and the order in which it is done is something known to every cat:

Paws, face, ears, chest, back, tail, tummy, bottom.

Licking a paw at least three times then washing the face and ears is highly effective, as all cats know too – our mothers teach us this. Or, if they are not there, we learn it from other cats. It is how we keep ourselves looking so beautiful and clean.

Appearances matter!

Any spare time – in this busy cat schedule – is spent sitting, or standing, and staring into space, which is very relaxing indeed – (you must try it!) – or playing.

Most cats can play happily with fallen leaves or twigs or insects we may find outside, or any objects really inside a house, such as toy mice or plastic balls or pieces of string or socks or, well, anything. Cardboard boxes are a particular favourite for games, and also double up as rather really good places to sleep.

It is when I am outside in the garden with Sami that it happens.

Shaheen is playing superheroes out on the street, running around laughing and smiling, with his red coat flapping behind him like a superhero cape.

It is so sunny and hot, with a beautiful big blue sky above, and lots of tweety birds singing.

The perfumed scent of the garden flowers hangs heavy in the air.

We do not expect the planes to come right then...

Suddenly, there is a loud growling roaring sound. It comes out of nowhere.

Three or maybe four planes fly over the house – fast and low.

And then, soon after, the bombs they have dropped explode:

BOOM BOOM BOOM BOOM!

THUD THUD THUD!

They do not fall on Sami's beautiful house, but explode not far away. We can hear buildings burst apart, and the crumbling of walls and houses, somewhere out there, in the street nearby.

I have jumped free of Sami and am hiding in my usual secret place in the garden.

I can hear my blood thump inside my ears, and can feel my heart pumping quicker in the terror.

Sami has rushed inside to be with her mum and dad. They crouch down under the dining room table as always during air raids.

More firework noise and bad burning smells.

BANG BANG BANG!

Then, quite suddenly, everything is quiet.

An eerie silence replaces the screeching and exploding of bombs.

I can hear some distant screaming and humans crying.

Slowly, and somewhat nervously, Sami comes out into the garden to be with her parents.

"Shaheen," she whispers. "Mum...dad... Where is Shaheen?"

It does not take us long to find him.

CHAPTER FIVE

As many of you may already know, we cats have nine lives. We are lucky.

Two-legs – humans – have just the one. They are not.

And I must say that, as a cat, I always find it surprising how so many of them seem to waste the one life they do have by worrying and being unhappy and fighting all the time.

Just like this awful war.

Sami and her parents are out.

It is Shaheen's funeral today.

We found him on the road, not very far from the house at all.

He was just lying there on the pavement, surrounded by rubble.

It was strewn everywhere when a bomb blew apart a building nearby – lumps of concrete, twisted metal and broken glass.

Shaheen didn't look injured – just asleep – with his red cape of a coat lying limp behind his little body, as lifeless as he was.

His parents rushed over and desperately checked if he was still breathing.

But it was no good, and there was no point taking him to hospital as it had been largely destroyed by the bombing too.

Sami stroked Shaheen's hair and found the place where something had hit his head. She lifted up her hand and showed her parents the blood on her fingers.

After Yousuf had carried his son's body into the house, he tried again and again to revive him with chest compressions, to make him breathe again, to make his still heart beat once more. But we all knew he had gone – over the two-legs rainbow bridge.

Everything was so sad. We cats cannot cry with our eyes, but do in our hearts at such times, though humans often do not realise. My heart was crying inside now, and I gave a low yowl of sorrow as I sat and watched the sadness all around.

Oh how I hated to see Sami and her parents so unhappy and distraught!

It was hours before they stopped crying.

There were no words.

There *are* no words.

Not human two-legs words – or cat miaow words either, come to that.

Sorrow hung heavy in the silence, which was interrupted only by sobs and wails, as Shaheen's mum, dad and sister mourned their loss.

Sami picked me up and hugged me, and I hugged her back.

There was nothing anyone could do.

We all felt so helpless – so useless.

I watched as Miriam hugged Shaheen's lifeless body, as if rocking him to sleep.

I remembered my lovely cat mum. I have very vague but happy and warm memories of her, from when I was a little mewling kitten, drinking the rich, delicious milk she made and gave me, and my kitten brothers and sisters. I remember her lovely mother-love smell.

The bond between a mum and her babies is so strong.

A while later, a woman and a man came to the house.

They washed Shaheen's body, brushed the concrete dust from the bomb blast out of his hair, combed it neatly. When that was done, they covered his face and body in a white shroud.

There were whispered words between Yousuf and Miriam and the woman.

Then the man and woman took Shaheen's little body away in a black car.

It was over.

I will miss Shaheen – his smiling face, his superhero games, his laughing. I shall even miss him pulling my tail – sort of, anyway.

I'll just miss him being there.

Poor Shaheen.

"It would have been quick," Sami's dad says quietly later, staring at the floor. "Just a bang on the head, and then...just...gone."

He puts his head in his hands.

No-one says anything.

Sadness lingers in the house like a bad smell.

No-one has any dinner to eat that evening – apart from me. Sami has put out some cat biscuits – I knew she wouldn't forget.

Yousuf looks at Miriam and nods. They both look at Sami.

She knows immediately what this means – the family will be leaving soon. They have to get out, or they will all end up like Shaheen.

They have no choice.

"But what about Summer?" says Sami, and they all look at me.

I miaow a miaow of comfort and understanding back. I know the family have to do what they have to do.

"We must get out while we still can, Sami," says her mum.

"We should have left before," says Yousuf, "but they are bad men, Miriam, very bad people, criminals and..."

"I know," says Miriam, reaching out an arm and touching her husband's shoulder tenderly. "It is not your fault, or anyone's fault, Yousuf."

And then he sobs – deep uncontrollable sobs from deep within. I have never heard Sami's dad make this sound before.

The next day, two men come to the house. One is thin with a nasty scar across his face; the other is fat and has a big beard with bits of old food in it. They both smell bad. I hide under a chair and pretend to be sleeping, but watch what is going on, as always.

Yousuf talks to the men. Miriam is there too. But Sami is not – her mum has sent her to her bedroom.

Then Sami's dad gets a plastic bag from a sideboard cupboard and hands it to the nasty-looking thin man.

"Half now, half later," Yousuf says.

The thin man counts the banknotes and sniffs.

The fat man nods:

"Tomorrow," he says. "Be ready. We will not wait."

Then they leave.

No-one says a thing. Sami comes into the room and her parents tell her they are all leaving their home – leaving Syria – the next day.

"We must all bloom where we are planted," says her dad. "Life goes on."

Her mum smiles sadly at him and nods.

Then everyone, including me, looks at Shaheen's red coat hanging up on a peg by the door.

I can smell the broken hearts in the room.

That evening, Sami and her parents pack their bags.

"One bag each," says Miriam.

I walk around the house with Sami and her mum, as they look around and try to decide what they want to take with them.

Sami picks up one of Shaheen's toys.

Her mum shakes her head.

"Only what we need – clothes, shoes, soap, toothpaste, my jewellery...maybe one or two books."

Sami always has her face in a book!

She picks up a photo of the family taken in the garden the previous year.

Shaheen is there, in his red superhero coat cape, and everyone is smiling.

And I am there too, in Sami's arms, purring, and looking very pretty and sweet, even if I say so myself.

Of course, nobody had a clue what was to come when that photo was taken.

Poor Shaheen...

Sami's mum nods and smiles at her daughter.

"Yes," she says, "we will take some photographs."

I miaow, and Sami picks me up and hugs me.

I hug her back.

I know this will be our last night together for a very long time.

CHAPTER SIX

The next morning, I wake up on Sami's bed.

I am not usually allowed to sleep upstairs – Sami's mum doesn't like cleaning up all the fur, she says.

But it's not my fault I moult!

Humans shed their skin too – and that is mostly what makes dust.

And there has been some dark talk of fleas – apparently Sami found one on her ankle, biting her – though why they assume I am to blame for that, I do not know.

Anyway, I wake up and nuzzle Sami's pretty face and long dark hair until she wakes up too. I purr loudly in her ear as she opens her eyes. She smiles through a yawn.

Then her smile wilts when she remembers what day it is – the day when she and the whole family will leave their home – without Shaheen. The day when they will be saying goodbye...

After breakfast – and Sami's mum gave me some cold chicken especially, as a treat – the cat box is brought out.

Usually, this appears only when I have to go to the vets – and especially back when I was a kitten-cat.

But we weren't going there today.

Sami smiles at me, picks me up and hugs me. I tickle her with my white whiskers and nudge her with my little white paws. She strokes my lovely ginger fur and hugs me closer.

"Sami," says her mum. "It's time."

I get into my box and Sami closes the metal grill door. I lie down, my paws tucked under me and look out.

I am not worried – I trust Sami and her family. I know what they are doing is for the best. I know they would take me with them if they could.

Sami and her parents walk to the cat shelter – it is not far away. I know where it is, of course, and am on fairly friendly terms with many of the residents already.

Sami carries the cat box, chatting to me on the way.

It is early, with a bright sun rising in the big blue sky – it'll be hot later. I can hear tweety birds singing on the way, and smell all sorts of smells – the bitter stench of burning from the bombs lingers in the air everywhere now.

Then we are there. My nose twitches and tickles at so many cat smells wafting all around me.

"Thank you, Abdul," Yousuf says to the handsome man who runs the shelter.

He has large sad eyes and a big bushy moustache, and smells kind.

"Yes, thank you," says Miriam. "We don't want to leave her – Summer – but..."

"I know," says Abdul, sadly. "Please do not worry – all cats are welcome here."

I like Abdul – he is so kind and gentle. If only all two-legs could be like him.

I remember Sami's dad talking about him before, how people treated him badly in his past life, and how that made him really love animals, and especially cats. He seems like a very wise man.

Then comes the moment I have been dreading – it is time to say goodbye.

Sami gets me out of the cat box and I hug her with my little white paws.

"Oh Summer, Summer," she whispers, kissing my fur, "I will miss you so much."

I miaow back that I shall miss her too, every day.

"I will never forget you, and I promise we shall meet again, after the war, when we come back...."

I miaow that I shall never forget her or Shaheen or their parents.

I promise that we shall meet again one day, no matter what – and that I shall find her, wherever she is.

I make a promise on my paws – and that is the biggest promise any cat can make. And we cats keep our promises – always.

I also make a wish on my whiskers, and hope it comes true.

There are tears rolling down Sami's cheeks.

I am crying inside, and my heart aches.

We touch noses to say goodbye, then Sami sets me down.

I stand at the feet of Abdul, by the door of the shelter.

Sami and her parents start off on their walk back to their home. I watch them as they leave.

Sami keeps on turning back to look at me, waving goodbye. She is in tears.

I raise my paw to wave goodbye to her too, and miaow a miaow of sorrow.

Then I lift my tail into a question mark and move my ears, left and right – Sami loves my tricks.

She smiles slightly, and oh so sadly, as she turns to look at me one last time.

Then she turns a corner and is gone.

My heart aches – I already miss them, especially Sami, my special two-legs.

CHAPTER SEVEN

In the shelter, I say hello to the cats, most of whom I know or have seen around.

"Hello," says a very pretty little sand-coloured cat with, I notice, only three legs.

"I'm Honey."

"I'm Summer," I miaow, and we sniff and nudge each other, then touch noses.

I have never seen Honey out and about and she tells me why.

"It is dangerous out there, with bad two-legs."

I tell her that she can come outside with me and that I shall keep her safe.

Honey's ears perk up at that, and she rolls on her back to thank me with her tummy fluff exposed.

Then Abdul comes in and feeds us all. Just basic cat biscuits from great big bags. Not as nice as Miriam's home cooking, but I do not complain. Many out there have nothing to eat at all, and some poor cats have never known a loving family in a *furever* home either.

Some cats appear from nowhere only when food is served. They do not live here, and many have *furever* homes but just like roaming, sometimes for days and even weeks, enjoying the hospitality of strangers.

We cats refer to such wanderer cats as:

'Missing, Presumed Fed'.

They usually go back home, and then often get extra treats from their relieved two-legs owners who have been worrying themselves sick! Clever, eh?

There must be over a hundred cats here. I am wary of some, especially the big toms. We she-cats stick together for safety, always.

But later that morning, after our post-breakfast nap, I make friends with some tomcats – Nook, Mo and Penguin.

And so we all go out on patrol together.

Honey has come out with me too and, although nervous at first, she is clearly enjoying all the new smells as we investigate the area.

Mo tells me there are some bad humans around now who are so hungry and desperate they will even try to catch cats to cook and eat!

Can you *imagine?*

So we avoid two-legs whenever we smell them, which is long before they see us: humans have a very primitive sense of smell, and their hearing is laughably bad. I don't know how they manage to survive at all sometimes, I really don't.

Penguin and Nook point out an old skinny woman from a distance – she has a net on a pole as she walks around the bomb site, trying to catch cats or rats or anything, for some meat to eat.

Just trying to survive, like the rest of us.

Honey catches a big black beetle! She may have a leg missing but it does not hold her back at all.

She crunches her creepy-crawly snack with a satisfied purr.

I find a big fat spider in the rubble – very tasty.

Yum-Yum!

When we get back, Abdul gives us all a cuddle and a hug – somehow he remembers all our names. He does this for every one of the cats at his shelter, which I know means a lot to us all.

Even better, he seems to have no two-legs friends, so we do not have to worry about any unwelcome human visitors.

But the war continues, and every few days the big metal birds – planes – come again and drop their bombs.

Then, one day, the worst thing happens: the cat shelter gets a direct hit and is destroyed.

BOOM!

All gone.

Flattened.

Blown apart.

I was lucky in a way – I was outside the shelter at the time, on patrol.

Many cats were not so lucky, including poor Honey – who was not with me that afternoon – and many other friends.

And there is no sign of Nook, Mo or Penguin – or Abdul – at all.

I wander through the smoke, away from the ruined cat shelter, and hide in the corner of the blackened concrete shell of a derelict building.

I am coughing and wheezing.

I feel tired and weak.

There is a stabbing pain in my neck.

I lift my paw up to it.

It feels wet.

Blood.

I lie down and curl up in a corner.

I now start to feel very cold.

But then I think of Sami, and Shaheen, and all my family in my *furever* home.

I think about their love, about how Sami loved me – and loves me – and hugged me ever so tight.

About her promise to meet again – and about my promise to find her again, no matter what.

About the wish I made on my whiskers and paws.

I am purring to ease the pain, much as humans groan to do the same when ill, injured and hurt.

And then I feel a wave of warmth wash over me, and I know all will be well. It is hard to explain.

My breathing is now becoming shallow and rapid.

I feel overwhelmed with fatigue, and begin sinking into sleep.

A dark, silent sleep.

And then all the pain is gone.

And the world is calm and comforting.

I can see Sami's face smiling at me... and I know –

I just know –

Everything is going to be alright.

And then my life dissolves –

Into a warm and gentle memory of love.

CHAPTER EIGHT

I wake in a world of white.

I have just enjoyed a long restful sleep, in the back of a sleigh in the snow.

I remember back to when I was reborn here and the moment I realised, with something of a jolt, that I was a little kitten again.

Black.

And male.

This came as something of a shock, I can tell you!

This is only my second life, after all. I had never had the experience of being born again before.

It was sort of strange being reborn. But then it would, wouldn't it?

But now I am grown up, an adult tomcat, and so used to it all in my second life - my black furry fur, my maleness, and of course the snow and the ice and constant cold of my new home in a place called Greenland.

It is no problem really, because we cats can survive anywhere - here, where the temperature is always below freezing, or in the hottest of hot scorching places on earth, like deserts or jungles.

So long as we get adequate food, clean drinking water and can find a quiet corner to have a wash and sleep, we cats are happy enough anywhere.

I have been living here over two years now, with my two-legs called Jonah, an Inuit fisherman. He is a kind human, and I serve him well, keeping him company on fishing trips out on the ice.

I am also there for his wife and two daughters in the small, warm wooden house where we all live. The young two-legs children like playing with me in the evenings, which I like too, as long as it's not when I want to sleep!

The climate here did take some getting used to at first. It is so freezing cold always that I can see my breath billow like smoke in the air whenever I am outside. And everything is frosty – with ice, hard and see-through, glinting like glass everywhere.

But, as I have said, we cats are born survivors and never complain. Dogs, well – what do you expect from such a doolally species? But we cats – never!

I am a well-padded, strong tomcat with a lovely thick coat of fur, so I can thrive out here.

I was the tiniest sausage of a kitten when I was born, as were my brothers and sisters – hardly able to move and completely unable to see. We kittens do not open our eyes for a week or more after birth.

Our sense of smell and hearing is there from the moment we are born though, and that is all we need to bond with our mum and suckle her for the rich delicious milk she makes for us.

After some weeks, Jonah came and selected me as the kitten he wanted to adopt and take home. He said I was the cheekiest and naughtiest one there. I don't know what he means!

He named me Shadow, which I like. It's sort of mysterious – though my real name will always be Summer. To me, anyway.

So now, here I am, a full-grown adult tomcat, brave and handsome, sleek and fast, with the sharpest of razor-sharp claws – and a loyal companion to Jonah.

Today, we are out fishing. I am lying down in the back of the sleigh as Jonah makes an igloo – a little round house entirely made of blocks of ice and compacted snow. He cuts them from a bank of exposed ice with a great big knife, then arranges them in a circle and builds on top of them, with more ice bricks, eventually making a dome shape.

I am with the huskies who pull the sledge. They are not very intelligent animals – well, they are dogs! – but they are pleasant and friendly enough, and I like them. Though I shall never understand their need to follow orders and work together as a team, copying what all the others do.

It is the opposite of cats, for we are all born individuals. We walk alone and do our own thing, always.

If you ever meet a cat who does *not* do that, then *please* be very careful, because it is most likely a dastardly imposter, and not a cat at all! Probably just a very jealous dog in disguise. Envy can be a terrible thing...

It is my duty to look after Jonah, and that is what I am doing as I lie down on the sleigh, watching him build an igloo. We cats are good at watching humans work.

I love work. I could watch it for *hours!*

I shall sleep in that little igloo house of ice with him tonight, inside in the toasty warm, away from all the cold and snow. The huskies will not be so lucky, as they have to stay outside huddling together in the snow to keep warm – but they are well used to it. Jonah feeds them well and they know it.

I help Jonah when he makes holes in the thick ice through which he drops fishing lines. I cannot, of course, drill holes in the ice myself – my claws may be sharp, but are not the right shape for doing that! And I leave all the fishing lines and baiting the hooks to my human too.

But I am the best there is at sensing danger. As you already know, cats have a superb sense of smell and hearing - unlike humans. So my job is to listen and sniff the air for any possible danger or threat.

I may have freezy ears as I stand in the snow, but they still work wonderfully well, as does my sensitive nose. I smell everything, and will shout out miaows loudly if I smell the faintest scent of polar bear.

If I indicate that one is in the area, then Jonah has a choice: stay here and get ready with the gun he always carries on his shoulder, or leave. He has always chosen to vacate the area on all previous occasions I have smelt bear.

Jonah loves all animals, even big and dangerous polar bears with paws and claws bigger than those of even the biggest of cats, so would never want to shoot one dead, or even injure it. We can all share this place, if we are careful and give each other space, consideration and respect.

But there is no bear smell twitching my nostrils today – just the stink of the fish bait Jonah puts on the hooks.

When he has done that, he feeds the huskies and me – lovely fresh fish! Then we sit on the back of the sleigh and Jonah sighs as we watch the sky darken. He drinks something from a flask but he does not offer any to me, which is fine – I only drink water really, and only very occasionally milk or cream as a treat.

"Oh Shadow," he says, smiling into my yellow eyes and stroking me. "Oh, my poor brother – he go out on fishing trip and never come back. Who know what happened? I miss him."

I sense his sadness so nuzzle his arm, and chirrup to comfort him. I do my tail question mark trick too, and move my ears, and cross and uncross my paws to try and cheer him up. It doesn't work.

"The ice sheet, it get thinner every year – the global warming, they are say, melting it – so he maybe fall through ice, or perhaps polar bear get him..."

He takes another swig from his flask and lets out a large gasp of a sigh.

We cuddle together and look up at the night sky, so full of countless twinkling stars, a canopy of bright diamonds sparkling up there with the moon.

Then there is the usual weird green lightshow glow in the sky. Jonah calls this the Northern Lights, and another name in the Inuit Greenlandic language.

It is a bit like watching that thing called television that two-legs like to gawp at for hours, except high in the sky and not in a box or an oblong screen.

It all makes me feel like a very small cat indeed.

CHAPTER NINE

The next morning is beautiful – with a big blue sky high above, and all around the ice and snow sparkling and glittering like diamonds.

There was a big blizzard during the night, when I was snug and warm with Jonah.

With blizzards, the wind is so cold it cuts through you like a claw. So I am grateful to my human for making the igloo.

The huskies were outside all night long in the freezing cold, but seem weirdly cheerful about it. Right now, they are enjoying their breakfast, as am I.

Jonah is drinking the hot drink he has boiled up.

I sniff the wind, which is light today. No scent of polar bear at all, though I do hear something – under the ice. This could be anything – an old Greenland shark drifting along, a big shoal of little fish perhaps, or a whale or two, or seals.

Whales and seals can hold their breath a long time, but have to come up for air eventually.

The whales – including killer whales, and narwhals with their one long 'unicorn' horn on their heads, and the snow-white beluga whales – breathe through their blow-holes when out in open water. But the seals often appear in holes in the ice to snort their nostrils and take another breath, which is when we see them.

Sometimes the hunters manage to catch a seal. They use it all for food, making clothing from its skin and using the blubber for heating oil. Nothing is wasted – nothing at all. Even the bones are cooked up for soup and then sometimes used for the men and women to make Inuit carvings which they then sell on to the tourist shops in the towns.

I help Jonah check the many fishing lines he dropped through ice holes the evening before, padding through the snow beside him. Some have wriggling fish on, but not all.

"Fishing better further up there, Shadow, but ice so thin now, it too dangerous," he says, sadly.

I miaow back in agreement.

"It never like this in old days. Back then, it colder with ice thicker – safe."

I miaow that it is perfectly cold enough as it is, thank you, but I can see his point.

When Jonah takes a break, I decide to slide down a big bank of snow.

Such fun!

Weeeeeeeeeee!

We cats like playing games – snow and ice are good for that sometimes.

Everything here – at least everything that lives on the land and not in the water – relies on the ice being frozen. If the ice gets too thin or melts altogether, then polar bears and other animals cannot walk on it or hunt. If that happens, they starve.

And Inuit fishermen cannot go out fishing either.

No ice = no life.

There are lots of ice holes to check, and I stay by Jonah's side, protecting him, on the alert for any and every threat or danger my wonderfully sensitive nose and ears tell me may be out there in the snow.

And then I smell something.

A familiar smell somehow.

Not polar bear, thankfully.

I try to identify it.

My nose twitches like a rabbit's and my ears rotate and scan the landscape in all directions for the slightest of sounds.

Then it comes: laughing.

I can hear laughing, very quiet at first and distant, then louder and closer.

There is someone else out here on the ice!

I miaow to Jonah, but not too loudly, as this is no polar bear danger alert.

He looks at me quizzically, then goes back to pulling in the fishing lines. I realise he cannot hear any laughing. But I can.

Then I see it.

A flash of red running around on the ice.

And I remember:

Shaheen!

He is running around playing superheroes with his red coat flying behind him like a cape, giggling with glee at the joy of it all.

Oh, how I remember his happy laugh!

And Sami too – the memory of her eyes. Her beautiful green eyes.

The almost-forgotten memories of my first life come flooding back to me, flowing through my eyes and mind like a waking dream or a film being replayed.

But how can this be? Shaheen was...

I do not understand, but do not have to. Seeing Shaheen there has made me remember.

He is some way off but sees me – I miaow a 'hello' at him and raise a paw. He laughs and waves back.

I now know what my purpose is: to find Sami and look after her. This is my duty as a cat.

Shaheen is not alive, but Sami is – and this is what I am being told, I know.

We all have a purpose in life – a reason why we are here.

And this is mine.

MY PURPOSE.

I feel my heart swell with warm certainty as my destiny becomes clear.

The next thing I know, Jonah is yelling:

"Seal!"

And there she is, her pretty whiskery, big-eyed head poking through an ice hole to breathe, nostrils flaring in the cold.

But before Jonah can get to her or fire his gun, she disappears back down into the cold black water.

Jonah curses, then runs over to the ice hole where the seal appeared.

"We make more ice hole, Shadow," he shouts. "Seal come back!"

I follow him further out onto the ice to drill more holes in it.

It is when he is scraping away, widening another new ice hole – and this one is further out on the ice than I have ever been – that I hear it.

The earth is groaning, as if in pain. A low growl, a bit like we cats make when we are ill or annoyed. A warning…

Jonah is too busy crunching away with his hand-turned drill making the ice hole to hear it. I miaow loudly and paw his legs. But by then, it is too late.

Suddenly, the groaning becomes louder.

And then, there is a new sound of creaking and cracking, and splitting and breaking.

I look around me in all directions.

Cracks appear in the ice, travelling along it like lightning, and all ending up where Jonah and I are standing, as if we are at the centre of a huge icy spider's web which growing all around us, and under our feet.

And then it happens.

The thin ice breaks.

CRRRACK!

And we fall through the ice into the water.

The sea is so cold, it almost burns.

We rise to the surface in shock, having had our heads submerged in water so unbearably cold it is a wonder anything can live in it.

Jonah is gasping and holding on to the surface ice. I do the same.

But the ice moves – it is all broken up, like little icebergs. We cannot pull ourselves out.

The huskies bark. I see them some way off – we really have travelled a long way from our usual fishing place.

They are safe there, I know.

We, however, are not.

Jonah and I are both shivering and shaking now, and our breathing is becoming faster as we gasp for air.

The water is so cold, I can hardly feel my paws.

I look at my human and muster just enough energy for the smallest of miaows.

Jonah's teeth are chattering. He smiles weakly back.

"Sorry...Shadow..." he gasps, in a whisper. "Ice...too thin...I sorry."

I open my mouth to miaow back that I forgive him, but nothing comes out – I am too weak, and now feel so tired and sleepy.

I see the seal poking his head above the ice some way off, in another ice hole Jonah made, its big black eyes staring blankly back at me.

I look over to the huskies who are whimpering as they watch.

I try to miaow to them to tell them everything will be alright, that people will come for them.

And then, I sink down into the cold black water with Jonah, never to be seen again.

CHAPTER TEN

It is *so* hot!

And I mean **HOT, HOT, HOT!**

I am in a place called Australia, in the Outback, surrounded by red, parched sand in a flat landscape which goes on forever in every direction, though there are a few rocks and trees and bushes around to explore – which I will surely do, because...

I am a newborn kitten in my third life.

My fur tells me that both I and my brothers are tabby cats, with stripes of light and dark brown all over our bodies.

I am smaller than them – the littlest kitten of all.

They call me the 'runt of the litter'. I am often the last to the milk because they push me out of the way – which is just their kitten instinct and nothing personal, I know. But my mum always makes sure I stay longer than the others, so get as much goodness from the nutritious rich milky food she makes and gives us.

And so, I grow – getting bigger and stronger day by day.

Our mum also helps all us kittens relieve ourselves and shows us how to keep clean, as all of our noble species should.

A clean cat is a happy cat.

She teaches me how to wash and makes a game of it, which is fun!

I love my mum, and snuggle up to her, all soft and warm and cuddly.

Even though here in the desert it is horribly hot in the daytime, it can get very cold at night, so snuggling keeps us all warm.

My mum cat teaches us how to hunt, lying in wait for beetles and flies, or maybe just dead leaves and twigs for practise, then jumping at them with our needle-sharp kitten claws to hold them down like mice. There is no escape!

Importantly, she also teaches us how and where to find water – in the most secret of places where liquid bubbles up from underground, or in the succulent, juicy plant leaves or stems we can chew on if we have to, or where two-legs dig to find water.

We have to be careful around them, and all other animals. But once humans have dug a water hole and drunk their fill, they move on – so we cats make the most of it and drink our fill too.

I also play with my brothers – we ambush and hunt each other. No-one ever gets *really* hurt. If we go too far, one kitten will yelp and yowl and the other will stop. Or sometimes, our mum will tell us off before we get too boisterous and rowdy.

My mum feeds and protects me, and teaches me to hunt, and everything else I know. And I work hard at being the best cat I can be to make her proud too.

But then, when I am about six months old, my mum goes out hunting one morning…

And she never comes back.

A fellow feral cat tells us nastily with a sneer that she'd seen our mum flattened and dead on the busy road where great big wheel-boxes drive by all day and night – huge long lorries and loaded trucks.

We chase her away. Some cats can be cruel like that.

I hate bullies!

But I know what my mum would have said – that as long as you behave with courtesy and manners like a well brought up cat, then you can survive any attack anyone ever makes on you.

You can even turn negative energy into positive energy – use negative criticism and insults as fuel to make you stronger.

And if you don't believe me – *just try it!*

Of course, those bad cats have not had the benefit of a proper upbringing with a loving cat mum – and it shows. So they are nasty out of envy really, which is sad, when you think about it. I feel sorry for them – mostly.

But I have to accept that my mum has gone...

I shall miss my lovely mum terribly – I loved her so much. But she is with me in my heart, I know, and always will be, guiding me with her wisdom and love.

The other animals here in Australia are just *amazing!*

And I mean:

AMAZING!

My favourites are the hoppity ones! I have fun hopping behind the kangaroos and wallabies in a line with my brothers.

Bouncy bouncy bouncy bouncy!

Hop hop hop!

I don't *think* they mind. They've never *said* anything anyway...

Then there are all the squawky birds in such wonderful colours, though the big tall walking ones called emu can be dangerous. We hide whenever we see them. A kick from one of those big birds can easily kill a cat.

At night, we hunt, but we are also careful, particularly of the wild dingo dogs – their eyes shine red in the darkness, like demons, so we can spot them easily. If there are too many red eyes shining back, we run and hide. A pack of dingoes can kill anything – and will, given half a chance.

We are also wary of snakes and spiders, especially – but not only – the most colourful ones. Our mum taught us never to play with them. Cats who do may well never play with anything ever again.

So many animals are poisonous here. And deadly.

But others are not, and I do love sniffing and snuffling around the red sand and bushes to find some of the funniest little creatures, like lizards.

The lizard with the frilled neck looks so funny, and the thorny one too. I don't get too close though, and avoid the bigger lizards completely as they are so scary to us kitten-cats and could easily eat us all up!

Insects are a big part of our diet here, together with mice and other small mammals and birds.

Beetles are a crunchy treat, as are the safer spiders, and grasshoppers.

Ants are tasty too, if a bit fiddly and tickly.

We often find them when we spot and follow a spiny ant eater – an echidna –then watch it find and dig up an ants' nest with its long pointy claws.

After a while, when the echidna has eaten all it wants, we cats and kittens move in and use our rough tongues to scoop up the ants – though only if they are not stingers!

We haven't really got the right tongues for it, to be honest, unlike the professional ant eaters who have very long sticky tongues indeed.

But we manage, if a little messily, to eat enough ants to fill our little bellies.

We have to spend a long time cleaning our fur coats whenever we have eaten ants. It's all very tricky really.

And if you don't believe me then you have a go at eating ants and see if you can do any better!

And this is how I have lived with my brothers and other feral cats, in the Australian Outback, surviving as best we can, avoiding humans and the wheel-boxes whizzing by, as well as the more dangerous animals and nastier cats.

Until one day, all that changed.

That was the day the bush fires came.

CHAPTER ELEVEN

I wake with the slightest hint of smoke smell tickling my nose.

It is early morning, and I see all my brothers and other cats are awake as they have smelt it too.

Of course, two-legs would not be able to smell such a small amount of smoke in the air – the human species is practically nose-blind, after all – but we cats can.

It immediately panics us all.

Fire is something we have learnt to be scared of, and for good reason.

In the Outback, which is so parched and dry, fires can travel fast – jumping from bush to bush, from tree to tree, even more quickly than the swiftest cat can run. A great many animals perish in them, though the plants and trees always seem to regrow from the ashes.

I sniff the breeze. It is sending confusing signals – as if the fire is coming from more than one direction.

I look at my brothers and yowl a question.

They yowl back.

Which way to run?

We cats are confused and do not like it – we do not like it one bit.

If there is danger, we need to know where it is – which is why we cats like to be up high, where we can survey the landscape and see everything.

But I have an idea.

There are trees not that far away – a wooded area. If I climb up to the top of a tree, I shall be able to see for miles around in all directions, and so identify where the fire is. Then we'll all be able to run in the opposite direction, away from the blaze and flames, to a safe place.

I put the idea to my brothers and other feral cats present. They all agree.

And so I head off, with brothers and others following behind me.

I am careful climbing the tree – not only because I have chosen the tallest and a fall could well be the end of a cat like me, even though I would surely land on all four paws. I may survive but...

No, I am also concerned about the creatures who live in the trees, especially snakes, who may well bite and would no doubt enjoy making a meal of a little kitten-cat like me!

But, what choice do I have?

I take three deep breaths, as my mum cat taught me to do in any challenging situations when I felt worried or nervous, and start to climb.

The sight that greets me when I am in the treetops, high above the ground, makes my heart sink. For the fire is all around – in all directions. It is still quite far away, but I cannot see a clear area free from fire where we can all run to.

The smoke smells stronger now – acrid and nasty in my nostrils.

I climb down – very carefully – and tell my brothers and others the bad news.

"The road," miaows one.

"But the wheel-boxes," miaows another.

"It's a risk we'll just have to take," I miaow back.

So we run as fast as we can to the big highway, where so many cats, including our lovely mum, have met their end. And many other unfortunate animals too.

The red dust from the desert is blowing in the strong hot wind. I have to squint to stop it getting into my eyes.

A rush of hot wind from the great big wheel-boxes – lorries and trucks – whizzing by tells me we have reached the road.

The scorching smell of fire is burning and hurting my nose now.

I try to run across the road, only for a big beast of a wheel-box to bear down on me, the beep blaring in my ears. I only just miss being run over by its huge wheels.

Confused, and disorientated, I just run.

I run and run and run!

Soon, I am surrounded by trees and bushes, all ablaze.

The flames crackle and dance, and the fire pops.

The inferno roars like it's *alive!*

A big living monster of furious flames and scorching heat at its heart, hungry for everything – anything – it can set alight and destroy.

I breathe in the heat and run round in circles, but there is no escape.

I am surrounded by a ring of fire, trapped.

I can feel it singeing my whiskers.

And the bitter smoke stings my eyes.

The entire world is being swallowed by the flames.

I sigh sadly and resign myself to my fiery fate. So I sit down on my sore and burnt paws, head hanging down to the ground.

I close my eyes and let out a long yowl of pain.

Just then, I hear laughing through the loud bush fire growl.

My pointy ears prick up.

More laughing – and giggling.

Shaheen!

I look up and there he is, running around with his red coat cape flapping behind him like a superhero.

He looks right at me and smiles. I know he wants me to follow him.

I do so, and soon I am running through a gap in the fire, then out into the desert and towards a rock where I know there is a water hole.

That is the last thing I remember.

I never see my brothers again.

The next thing I know, I am with an old man who has very dark skin and black hair with some white in it.

He is changing the bandage wrapping on my paws, smearing them with some strong-selling creamy mixture he has made in a bowl from herbs and plants and other things.

I do not know why, but I automatically trust him.

The old man smiles at me.

"G'day," he says as I squint at his friendly smiling face, "I gonna call you Kimba, which mean 'bush fire' in Aborigine language."

We touch noses. Not many humans do that, but this one does.

"You're a beauty, ain't ya? I'm Lenny. Stoked to meet ya, Kimba!"

From that point on, I live with Lenny in his camp. Other humans live there, but I stick with Lenny. We share everything.

I often go with him into the Outback, tracking animals, hunting, or collecting herbs, plants and berries for food or medicine. Or sometimes doing dot paintings on rocks.

Lenny shows me paintings his ancestors have drawn thousands of years ago.

He then does hand paintings on the rock surface and shows me how to do paw paintings.

You should try it!

It's great fun, though perhaps a little messy, and I have to wash my paws a lot afterwards.

Lenny says these hand and paw prints will last for thousands of years too.

I miaow happily, then do my question mark tail trick, and move my ears, and cross and uncross my paws to make him smile.

Lenny doesn't talk much, especially to other two-legs. I do not mind at all, and think he is very wise to be like this.

I have often noticed how a great many people talk to each other all day long without having a clue what they are really saying to each other. It's very odd to watch, and worse to listen to.

Lenny talks more to me, actually, than to any of his own human species.

And I talk back to him – in miaows and chirrups, and yowls and purrs.

And he understands too!

This is simply marvellous!

A great many two-legs fail to understand even the most basic of cat words. But then, it's not really their fault, I suppose – more a sort of design flaw in their inferior species. One mustn't mock...

Some of Lenny's tribal family members joke that we spend so much time together we should get married. Then they say, maybe not, because we get on far too well for that – which is a joke, apparently.

They laugh and laugh and laugh.

But we ignore them.

We are happy as we are, together alone, and live happily together for many years.

I live to a good age, and Lenny is a very old man when I finally fall asleep and slip away into my new life, somewhere in the stars.

CHAPTER TWELVE

My fourth life is very different.

I am living on an island full of cats – a *Nekojima* – in a country called Japan.

I have no given name, though the hundreds of cats here have their own names for themselves and each other – which humans cannot hope to understand.

I still call myself Summer though.

I always will.

I have no two-legs human to look after here either – none of us do.

But we live well here in our island colony of cats. The weather suits us – hot in summer, sometimes rainy too, but not *too* hot, and not too cold in winter either, when it is often sunny. We have empty huts and caves and cabins in which to seek shelter, from the rain or the heat, if we want.

We often sleep through it, which is a good cat way of coping with a great many difficult situations – and a good thing too!

This island is one where no humans live, but many fishermen have long used it to land and clean their fish after being out at sea. That means that we cats eat very well indeed! All sorts of fish species that the fishermen catch.

They give us the parts they do not sell or eat – the fish heads, for example, and all the guts and innards.

Yum-Yum!

Nothing is ever wasted.

There are all sorts of cats here – big and small, young and old, with every colour of fur imaginable, from black to ginger, to tabby to grey, to all shades of brown and white and orange.

I myself am white – except for my tail which is gingery-brown, and my ears and a patch on the top of my head between them which is the same colour. Apart from that, I am snow-white all over and a very pretty she-cat indeed – even though I say so myself!

This white coat would have been good camouflage in my second life in snowy Greenland, but we cats cannot chose such things.

Of course, our fur colour is always *purr-fect,* whatever it is – we cats are handsome and beautiful in any shade, as you already know.

And so we live happily here, on our cat island. There can be conflicts and arguments, from time to time, but we cats generally manage to avoid each other before any serious fights take place. There can, however, be a great deal of hissing and spitting at such times, and a lot of fur standing on end, as cats confront each other – but it always sounds worse than it is, and rarely ends in paws and claws and violence.

One day, when I was a kitten, I saw another cat who looked very similar to me – mostly white but with ginger-brown tail and ears. Her smell was somehow familiar.

It was when we touched noses that I realised who it was.

Honey!

The three-legged cat from the Abdul's shelter back in Syria.

She had been reborn in another life here too.

What a wonderful coincidence!

It's always great to see old friends!

"I have all four legs now, in this life," chirruped Honey, proudly waggling her pretty paws at me, front and back.

However, I noticed that the top parts of her ears were missing.

"The tips were white, and got sunburnt and sore," explained Honey, "so the vet, she snipped them off. I can hear just fine though!"

I know Honey says this, but in reality she is a bit deaf – though not because the tips of her ears are missing. I have to miaow and yowl and chirrup just that little bit louder so Honey can hear me.

Deafness is common in white cats, I know. Some are just born that way.

But not me – my hearing is *purr-fect!*

The vet comes out to the island from the mainland every couple of months. She and her lovely assistants give us health checks and help any of us who seem unwell in any way.

I must say, they really are very good, and so knowledgeable about all matters feline. It pains me to say it in a way, because the two-legs species is so very inferior to our own. However, these humans are almost honorary cats – they like us so much and know all about how we live and think and behave. They're learning!

Some cats are nervous of strangers, and that is no wonder. But most – myself included – actually like saying a miaow-hello to the vet when she comes. She remembers us all too.

She always calls us 'beautiful cats'.

Well, we know we are!

Two-legs do have a rather tiresome habit of stating the obvious, I find – even this clever vet. I suppose they just can't help it, so I try the best I can to be understanding and tolerant of their many deficiencies, as all well-behaved cats must.

Manners maketh cat!

We get tourist boats visiting in season here – people of all kinds from all over the world speaking all sorts of funny-sounding human languages. So we are used to two-legs tramping around our island, and know they will not hurt us.

We pose for photos with them and they reward us with hugs and kisses – and, most importantly, tasty treats!

Looking back, being so trusting of strangers might not have been such a good thing, considering what happened later...

It is springtime now, and the cherry blossom season is here again. It is so beautiful, with the *sakura* trees flowering with their pretty pink blossoms everywhere.

There is a festival – *hanami* – where the local people have picnics and barbeques outside to celebrate the cherry trees flowering. This is a very good time for us cats as we get lots of titbits and scraps of what the humans are eating. Well, vets do recommend a varied diet!

And so, it happens...

We cats are so stuffed full of food that we are all sleeping it off, in our really deep sleep mode, for many hours afterwards.

This is perhaps why we are not as alert as we could be when they arrive – when the Chinese pirates come in their junks.

Their boats arrive quietly in the night.

Then they creep ashore from the beach, like crabs.

When we hear a commotion, we cats all wake up and run outside – straight into the trap.

There are nets set up across certain paths which snare and snag us.

Then the men shoot nets from cannons to catch more of us, like the way they catch birds – a particular humiliation for our proud cat species.

They discard the older and scruffier cats, who then limp off as quickly as they can, to hide somewhere safe and secret. I know they will survive alright.

But they do not let us go – we who are young and pretty, with soft beautiful furry coats. And, I notice, they particularly like the cats like me, and Honey, who have mostly white fur.

The pirates laugh nastily with sneery smiles curled on their greedy lips, especially when they grab any white cats out of the nets.

I know when these people put us in bamboo cages and load them on their boats that our happy life here is over.

But then, nothing lasts forever – not the cherry blossom, not the springtime, and not our lives on our beautiful *Nekojima* cat island.

CHAPTER THIRTEEN

I wake up on the high seas.

I am in a bamboo cage with Honey and several other white cats, all squeezed tightly together. Some are sleeping – or pretending to.

I look around.

Sea in every direction, like a big wet desert.

No land at all anywhere.

The whole boat is piled with cages stacked one on top of the other, and each one is crammed with cats.

Many are wailing and yowling. Some sit quietly, their heads in their paws, trying to wish the hurtful world away. The kittens are whimpering and squealing. It is a terrible, sad sound.

I try pushing the cage door with my head, put all my strength into it, as do Honey and other cats – but it is secured tightly and will not open, not even a bit. And the bamboo bars of our cages are too thick to bite and gnaw through. We are totally trapped.

"There is no escape, Summer," whimpers Honey, sitting down sadly on her four folded paws and lowering her head.

"We must never give up hope," I say to her, though I can see no way out of this either.

Honey falls asleep. I watch her dreaming, her little white whiskers and paws twitching as she dreams bad dreams. But they cannot be worse than the real-life nightmare we are now living through.

We have no idea where we are going, where we are being taken in our cages, or for how long we shall be at sea. We are journeying into the unknown.

I can see the Chinese pirates – several of them – drinking from bottles as they steer the boat. Some are singing drunkenly. They give us no food or water whatsoever.

And I can hear them laughing and joking about how much money they will get when they sell our fur coats. One says he is looking forward to drinking soup made from boiling us alive, saying how it will clean his blood and make him stronger. I shiver a little inside when I hear this.

I can smell these men too, unfortunately. They smell bad. They stink of greed and hate, like the very worst of their species.

The sea is becoming rough, with waves rocking the boat from side to side like a see-saw. Some cats are sick – they cannot help it – and the smell of it hangs in the air, despite the increasingly blustery wind.

We all have to relieve ourselves in our cages too, which for us cats – who insist on cleanliness at all times – is just awful. But we have no choice.

The sky gets darker and the sea gets even rougher. Big waves – the size of houses – are now crashing against the boat so hard I fear it may roll over, capsize and sink. That would be the end of not only us cats, but also our captors – so we have no choice but to trust them to save us all now.

The storm roars louder than an angry lion as we roll and sway in the swell, rain and sea water lashing us hard from all directions. The wind whistles and screeches as the typhoon rages around us – a sea monster swallowing us whole!

Then I can see the men steer the boat in another direction, and I feel us change course. We turn right, towards the only light in the sky – a yellowish-white gap in the clouds.

After a while, I can see land on the horizon. It is not our old home, of course – it looks very different, and much, much bigger. It is clearly not a small island.

As we get nearer, I can see there is a beach, then thick jungle, and far in the distance, a big mountain shrouded in mist. Who knows where we are?

At last, the boat reaches land. There is a natural harbour in the bay, and the wind drops as soon as we enter it.

There are no more massive waves rocking the junk dangerously any more – we are safe here. From the sea anyway.

The crew drop anchor and clamber into the shallow water then onto the land, leaving us cats in our cages on the boat.

Later on, they come back and carry us ashore. They take us to a clearing in the jungle where they pile up the cages. And they now give us water, throw buckets of it on us, so at least we can drink.

There is still no food though. We cats are all starving hungry.

Then they leave, heading off to a house I can see a long way off with lights in the window – no doubt this is where they will spend the night. I see there is a village beyond that, with houses and lights, which means other people.

I know we have to escape – and tonight.

By tomorrow, it will be too late.

We'll be back on the boat being taken to our destination and our doom, I am sure of it.

CHAPTER FOURTEEN

I try again and again, as hard as I can, to loosen the door of the bamboo cage, to break through it. But it is no good, and I collapse exhausted beside Honey.

She purrs at me and washes my head and ears, which comforts me a little. We slow-blink each other, touch noses, and fall asleep in each other's paws. We know that whatever happens, we shall be together.

Then, in the middle of the night, my nose twitches at a familiar smell.

Shaheen!

The door of the cage suddenly swings open.

I see a flash of red as Shaheen laughs and giggles as he runs off, playing superheroes again with his coat flapping behind him like a cape.

I jump out with the others from my cage and there are cats everywhere!

I can see several two-legs opening all the cages to free us. Local people, it seems. Most are female two-legs, and some are girls not much older than Sami was when I knew her.

These humans have similar facial features to the nasty pirates who stole us from our island. But they are not nasty – they are nice.

They are clearly cat lovers – so they're intelligent too, obviously.

And they want to free us!

I do not really know exactly who these nice, kind humans are, but I know they are our saviours – they are literally saving our lives.

These good people open all the cages and shoo all us cats into the jungle away from danger.

I miaow a loud thank you to them as I leave. I hope they hear me.

Then there is lots of loud yelling and shouting coming from the house – the pirates have heard us too. We have to move quickly.

"Run, cats, run!" I yowl as loud as I can, and we cats all run away into the jungle as fast as we can.

We all escape – no cat gets left behind, which is as it should be.

I see the local people standing up to the pirates and capturing them – and I watch them tying their hands behind their backs. A local policeman is there too.

I will be happy if these bad humans are stopped from ever stealing cats again. Who knows how many poor animals have been hurt by them already?

So now, many cats will be saved from slavery and protected from being stolen from their homes, because of what happened this night.

Hoorah!

In the coming weeks and months, we explore the jungle and find a place – a rocky cove – where fishermen come ashore to clean their catch.

Most cats decide to stay in this area due to the ready supply of fish bits – the yummy heads and guts – from these kind men, and the fact that the jungle both looks, and sounds, rather scary and dangerous.

I have never heard animal noises like it!

Some real monsters must live there – cat-eating monsters!

Though I have never actually seen one...

There are also comfy caves near the cove, some up in the cliff which are hard to get to, so very safe for us cats. We sleep soundly and eat well here.

And so our lives go on in this new place, for a good couple of years.

But it was not to last.

We both feel it when it happens, me and Honey. The low thud of vibration deep in the earth, early one morning.

Other animals hear it too. We are all good at sensing such things, unlike humans who seem to have no senses of any use at all. It's a wonder any of the two-legs species survive at all really.

They probably couldn't – not without our help!

Many small animals have already disappeared, and birds squawk in the tropical trees, then fly off inland, up to the mountain. The air is eerily silent and still.

I know what this is – an earthquake, far off, under the sea. I have known one before, on the cat island.

And when it happens, a big wave of water can come – a tsunami – which destroys everything in its path. Houses are smashed like matchsticks, wheelboxes – cars – are washed away, and any humans and animals who fail to escape it too. Nothing in its path survives.

"*RUN!*" I miaow loudly at Honey and any other cats who can hear me. "We must get to higher ground – the mountain!"

And so we run into the jungle, as fast as our little furry legs can carry us.

But Honey cannot run fast. She has been unwell for some weeks, getting gradually weaker. I do not know why.

After a while, she slows down and comes to a halt, panting and out of breath.

"You go on," she says, weakly and wheezing. "I'm not going to make it."

I slow down and stop running, then turn back to be with Honey.

"I shall stay here with you, no matter what," I say.

I chirrup at her and bow my head. Honey does the same. We touch noses and slow-blink, gazing into each other's eyes.

And so we lie down on a bed of leaves on the jungle floor, cuddling up together in one another's paws, purring our acceptance of the ways of the world as we wait for the huge wave of water to wash us away.

CHAPTER FIFTEEN

I am now in a land of plastic, in a place called Spain.

There are miles and miles of greenhouses which are made of see-through plastic sheeting, not glass. In them, all different kinds of colourful fruit and vegetables are grown.

I am a very handsome grey tomcat in this life, with an athletic build and the most beautiful orange eyes.

No wonder all the humans here love me!

I also catch a lot of mice.

The men who live in plastic land all have dark colour skins and are from a land called

Africa. They came here to work to make money, and spend all day long picking the fruit and vegetables. Every day is the same. Their lives are very hard.

Yumi is my two-legs. He walks with a limp and is one of the oldest workers. He often seems very tired but tries his best to keep up with the younger men, though that wears him out even more.

He is the one who found me when I was a kitten, out in the scorching countryside, when he was returning from a trip to the supermarket.

I was with my mum, and my brothers and sisters, but none of them survived.

Yumi nursed me back to health, feeding me with milk from a baby's bottle and keeping me warm, even taking me to the vets for a check-up.

So now I look after Yumi and stay by his side, in the run-down scruffy dormitory where all the workers sleep. The living conditions are awful, especially for humans.

There is just one smell-room – toilet – for them all to share, and no regular hot water, and just one shower too. For cooking, there is an old cooker with two rings and a gas bottle that the workers have to pay for out of their meagre wages.

Yumi calls me 'Lucky', because I was so lucky he found me and saved my life.

I like hunting very much. Yumi jokes that he should have called me 'Oringo' which is an African word that means 'he who likes to hunt'.

But I have to say I prefer 'Lucky'!

When Yumi is picking the vegetables all day long with the other men, I go on my patrols, exploring the many miles of plastic land. It is endless. I have never been outside it since Yumi found me as a kitten.

There are lots of mice around who feed on seeds, nuts and fruit, and any food waste the workers throw away. I get big and strong catching and eating them!

It all adds to the food I share with Yumi every evening, often a stew with rice or pasta. The African workers all cook together – they do not have much money for food and it is cheaper that way.

I have grown up in plastic land, so know everyone. Most of the workers like me very much.

But not all...

However, I know the ones who do not and avoid them.

At night, I curl up next to Yumi and keep him company. He talks to me a lot, about his family in Africa, his hard journey here, and about how he is getting old – and homesick.

"But I cannot go back – we cannot return – not like this," he says, wearily. "It would bring shame to our families, coming to Europe and not succeed. So we stay here – we are trapped."

I chirrup and miaow, and head-bonk Yumi to cheer him up.

Sometimes the foreman comes. He oversees the day-to-day work of the men here, and tells them what to do.

I do not like him – he smells bad. He has cold black eyes like a shark, a nasty thin smile curled on his face, and shouts a lot in Spanish with his big booming bullying voice.

He also carries a thin stick, something like a cane. He whips workers with it sometimes, to make them work faster, or for no reason at all. He seems to enjoy it.

But he usually goes away soon, off to the next plastic greenhouse to bark orders and bully the men there.

"Living in fear means not living at all," sighs Yumi, sadly, all the time.

One day, the men are ordered to pick aubergines and courgettes. There is so much produce growing here – tomatoes, cucumbers, various fruit and vegetables. The men pick them all, then box them up to be sent all over Europe – to Germany, Britain and elsewhere.

I can see Yumi is not well. He looks so tired and weary, with dull, distant eyes, and his limp is worse than ever. Humans cannot hide illness as well as we cats can.

But he has to work, he says, because:

"...if I no work, Lucky, I no get paid and we no eat good."

And so, he struggles on, working to a point of exhaustion, all day, every day.

I am concerned, so do not go out and about on patrol or on a hunting trip today. Yumi is my two-legs here, so it is my duty to care for him – though, of course, my main two-legs is Sami and my quest, as a cat called Summer, is to find her.

Today, the grey-haired and very fat besuited owner of plastic land visits. He arrives in a big shiny wheel-box with a driver and a very young female human dripping with jewellery in the back seat with him.

The owner gets out and walks towards the foreman. He is smoking a big cigar – what we cats call a 'smoke-stick'.

Yeeeuck!

Smoking is a very bad and disgusting human habit – one of many, and one of the worst.

It *stinks!*

The young female stays in the car and stares into a small mirror painting her face. I shall never understand the ways of two-legs as long as I live!

The African men work as hard and fast as they can. But Yumi just cannot keep up – just as I could not do much when I was ill as a kitten.

The foreman and owner walk into the plastic greenhouse together, watching the men slave away, picking the produce.

"Work!" yells the foreman. "Or...you want go back Africa?"

"No," groan some of them, though most keep their heads down and stay silent.

"Lazy savages! This not a holiday – you must to work. So WORK!"

The men pick the vegetables as fast as they can.

Then the foreman notices Yumi and walks right up to him, watched by the owner's beady eyes.

He yells and yells at him, and Yumi tries his best to work faster.

But it is not fast enough.

Then the foreman raises his arm and whips Yumi with the stick he carries.

Hard.

Yumi shouts out in pain – yelps like a puppy.

He is only wearing a thin white T-shirt, which is drenched with sweat in the heat.

He begs the foreman to stop.

But he doesn't.

He whips and whips Yumi, until he kneels, then falls to the ground.

I watch this with anger growing inside me like a ball of fire.

We cats respect the rule of law, yes.

But sometimes, in circumstances such as these, it is permitted for even the calmest cat to resort to:

The rule of claw!

It's all just a question of having the right *'catitude'*.

So, right then, I leap up onto the foreman's back and sink my sharp tomcat claws into the flesh at the back of his fat neck.

"*Yaaaaarrrrrggggghhhh!*" he screams. "Get it *off* me!"

But the other workers just watch.

They do not help the foreman.

They have seen him whip Yumi – and others too.

Instead, they go to Yumi and help him limp away, his arms over their shoulders.

One of them says the word 'hospital' and I know Yumi will be alright.

The owner, meanwhile, is so shocked at what has happened that the big cigar drops from his open mouth.

His girlfriend in the back of the car shrieks in horror.

"Get rid of that cat!" the owner yells while retreating back towards the car. "My girlfriend, she hate the cats."

"Yes, sir," gasps the foreman, who is turning around in circles with me still attached to his back with my claws.

He cannot get me off him.

I shall retract my claws only when I am good and ready.

Sometimes being a cat can be very satisfying indeed.

CHAPTER SIXTEEN

I know what's coming will be bad, and it is.

Eventually, I let go of the foreman's back, though I have clawed him so much his white shirt is stained red with blood.

Then I run away, as fast as I can – to get lost hiding in plastic land.

But, after three days on the run, a worker creeps up on me when I am dozing, grabs me by the scruff of the neck and throws me in a sack.

I hear the foreman's booming voice laughing nastily. He says the worker who found me will get a bonus.

He then beats the sack with his stick. I can feel which side he is hitting, so can move to avoid getting any damage to my head, though I do get bruised along my body.

I am carried off, a cat in a bag.

It is so dark in the sack – I cannot see out at all.

But I can hear, so know I am being put into a car boot.

I can also smell humans outside the bag, even though inside it pongs of rotten vegetables.

People always stink way more than they think!

The car is started and drives off.

After some time, we come to a stop. The door opens and someone – not the foreman, because I'd know his disgusting man-stink anywhere – lifts up the sack.

Whoever is carrying me walks for a while. I have no idea where we are now.

Then the sack is swung back and forth several times.

I feel giddy and sick and dizzy.

And then I am up in the air.

It feels as though I am floating – like a cloud or a balloon.

But I am actually falling...

The sack lands in what sounds like a tree.

I hear branches and twigs snap and splinter, the rustle of leaves, and the protesting squawks of tweety birds as I crash through the foliage.

Eventually, the sack hits the ground.

Everything is still.

Everything.

Silence.

I check myself all over.

No bones broken, thank goodness. I breathe a sigh of relief. Broken bones would mean certain death for a cat in my situation.

But I have a big problem: I am tied in a sack. If I cannot somehow get out, and soon, then I shall not survive.

I keep trying to scratch and bite my way out of the bag with my sharp claws and teeth. But it seems to have several layers and is made of thick material, so it hardly frays at all.

I focus on the tied opening to the sack, keep clawing away at it, biting it as hard as I can, all in the pitch darkness – and I do this for hours and hours, until I am totally exhausted.

The hunger gnaws at my stomach like a rat, but the thirst is worse. If I do not drink water soon, then I won't last very long, not in this scorching heat.

But I do not give up.

We cats never ever give up – that is one reason we are born survivors.

I sleep from time to time. Then, when I awake, I keep trying to open the sack over and over and over again.

I only know what time of day it is from how hot it is and whether the tweety birds are singing. They always make such a racket at dawn, and again in the evening before they go back to their bedtime nests.

I feel myself getting gradually weaker and weaker. This must be how Yumi felt, working away picking produce when he was so tired and ill.

The rest breaks I take between scratching at the inside of the sack with my claws get longer and longer.

I am so parched and thirsty, and my stomach aches with hunger. When I sleep, I dream of having a bowl of lovely clean fresh water to drink from and a tasty roast chicken dinner. My favourite!

Then I wake in the darkness, and realise it was all just a dream, and groan a low groan to myself.

I have never felt so alone in the world.

But I never give up.

I shall never give up.

Never never NEVER!

Then, one night when I am so weak I can hardly lift a paw, I smell a smell.

It is a smell I know too.

Shaheen!

Then, as if by magic, the sack is untied.

I struggle out through the opening and I am free!

I see Shaheen run off with his red coat flapping behind him like a superhero, laughing and giggling.

He stops and waves at me. I raise a paw back and do a silent miaow of thanks.

And then he is gone.

I find myself in a clearing in a forest. It is night-time, but we cats are really rather good at seeing in the dark.

My legs wobble a bit and I feel dizzy and weak.

I know I need to find water – and quick. Then food.

I look around me.

There!

I see water!

The moon is reflected on the surface of a small pond.

I walk to towards it – though I feel myself limping and cannot move fast.

I reach the edge of the pond. The water looks black and oily.

There are rusting wrecks of cars nearby, and old shopping trolleys and other junk that people have dumped there.

I have no choice but to drink the water, though it smells bad.

It tastes foul – dirty and disgusting and just so horrible. But I quench my thirst anyway. I have to.

I then follow a trail of trash and eventually arrive at a huge tip. I know that human rubbish often has leftover food in it, and so start sifting through it for anything I can eat.

I find lots of packaging with scraps of food left in or on it, and other edible waste.

So I eat and eat and eat – anything I can. It often smells and tastes bad, but we cats can cope with eating many things human cannot.

Anyway, I am starving, so have to fill my belly however I can.

Beggar cats can't be chooser cats!

I know I have become thin. I can feel my ribs poking through my skin, just like when I was an ill little kitten and alone.

And then I sleep, tucked up and hidden away in a broken plastic bucket I discover on the rubbish tip.

I wake the next morning to noise – large wheel-box lorries have arrived at the tip and are about to dump tonnes of rubbish right on top of me!

I limp away as quickly as I can, scuttling off like a beetle – albeit a slow and injured one. The rubbish dumped from the back of the lorries just misses me.

Eventually, I find a safe place to lie down next to an olive tree in a field nearby.

I feel very sick. I vomit on the ground and then relieve myself – a very smelly liquid deposit. I am too weak to cover it all up, so stagger away and slump down next to another tree in the shade.

I doze a while, then wake up and keep on walking. I know I have to keep moving – I have to find a source of clean water and food.

But then I smell a wonderful smell.

The most wonderful smell in the world.

FOOD!

Delicious food too!

I keep walking in the direction of the smell, and see a big road. Lots of wheel-boxes are parked in a lay-by, and some people are cooking meat on barbecues.

The smell of it is so gorgeous I almost faint with joy. My mouth waters as I breathe in the delicious scent.

I try to walk further, though for some reason my legs are not working well.

But I do not give up.

I keep walking with my back legs dragging behind me.

Eventually, I am by the side of the big road, in the lay-by where many cars and lorries have stopped.

The smell of food overcomes me and I faint, collapsing on the tarmac.

I drift in an out of consciousness, half-awake, half-asleep, like in a dream.

But when I look up, I see a bearded two-legs man-face looking down at me.

It is the last thing I remember.

CHAPTER SEVENTEEN

I wake in a place surrounded by the smell of cats and dogs – and goodness knows what else!

I have known this experience before, so I know where I am – at the vets.

"Will he be OK?" asks a voice.

I squint up to see the bearded man who found me at the lay-by, a concerned and kind look on his face.

The vet – a she-human – pokes and prods me a lot, and in some *very* intimate and delicate places, I must say.

But I know she means no harm and is trying to make me better. Also, I am too weak to protest or scram anyone in the state I am in. I am sicker than I first realised.

Actually, I really want to purr a 'thank you' to the bearded man and the vet, but cannot muster the energy.

"I give him some shots, antibiotics, vitamins – now he need only rest, fresh water, good diet...the love..."

"TLC, eh?" nods the man.

Tender – Loving – Care.

He then carries me away in a basket.

"Well," he says, "it looks like you're coming home with me then."

What luck!

I seem to have fallen on all four paws again!

One can never be too careful with two-legs, so to find two nice and kind ones in one lifetime is great good fortune indeed!

"I'm Huw, by the way," says the man, later on. "And we'll have to think about what to call you now, won't we?"

I try to tell him my name here is 'Lucky', though it was 'Summer' at first, then other names after that... but he doesn't understand me, as it comes out as:

"Miaow-miaow-yow-yow-miaow-yow-chirrup-chirrup-yowl-wow-wow-miaow-miaow-miaow-yowl-yowl-miaow-miaow-chirrup..."

"Talkative tomcat, eh?" Huw chuckles. "I bet you could tell some tales, boy?"

I am feeling tired so lie down in my basket by the window in the back of the camper van, looking out at the world passing by.

Then I see him –*Yumi!*

He is standing by a bus stop with two large bags by his side, waiting for the shuttle bus to the airport.

Yumi must be going home – to Africa – far away from that awful plastic land and the backbreaking hard work there. He looks happier than I have ever seen him before.

I place my paws on the window and miaow 'hello' and 'goodbye' at the same time, but he does not see or hear me. I hope he gets back to his forever home safely, to be with his family again.

I shall never forget Yumi – he saved my life, after all.

Now I am safe and sound once again, with a new two-legs to look after.

We drive a long way, sometimes stopping for the night in a place called France.

This is where Huw goes shopping and brings back long bread called 'baguettes' and very smelly, pongy cheese. I prefer the cold chicken and ham he gives me.

After two days, we are on a big boat – a ferry. Huw takes me outside on deck and I see sea all around me, until eventually I see land – the white cliffs of Dover, he says.

We drive ashore and continue on our way, driving west past lovely rolling hills and lush Kent countryside.

Eventually, after I enjoy a lovely long sleep for hours, we arrive in a place called Wales.

Then, after a drive down lots of twisty lanes, we arrive at a pretty little whitewashed house looking out onto a wide and beautiful blue-green sea.

And this is where I live now, with my new two-legs, Huw.

There are so many places here to explore – the countryside, with the funny woolly animals called sheep baaing everywhere, and of course the seashore too.

I love playing around on the beach, with the tickle of the wind on my fur, even when the wet crackle of the pelting rain fills my ears. After being stuck so long inside, back in plastic land, then outside in the scorching heat of Spain, I enjoy the freshness of the weather – it makes me feel alive!

Sometimes I catch and eat little fish from the rockpools, and occasionally I even find bigger dead fish washed up on the beach. If they haven't been dead for all that long, I eat them too!

But I have learnt from experience not to touch dead fish that is *too* old. The one time I did, I had the most terrible tummy rumbles and couldn't eat for two whole days afterwards, while I got better – and that, I have to tell you, is a real cat tragedy, as is any single day without food. I have learnt my lesson.

It rains a lot here – Huw says that is why the landscape is so lush and green – so it's a good job I have such thick and beautiful grey fur, I must say.

Sometimes I get so into my exploring that I do not hear Huw calling me. When I eventually come in, he always says:

Little cats good as gold, never doing what they're told...

I then chirrup and miaow happily back, and nudge his legs for food!

My new name is 'Merlin', by the way.

Huw says:

"Merlin was a Welsh wizard to the great King Arthur himself, from down there in Carmarthen – they say he was eventually imprisoned in a house of glass..."

I yowl – it doesn't sound very nice to be imprisoned anywhere.

"But you are free, Merlin – you're my little wizard cat who appeared like magic in my life," says Huw, "and to think I wasn't going to get any more cats, not after Leo left us."

Leo must have been his last cat – a cousin, no doubt – now gone over the rainbow bridge.

"Y'know I've always preferred the company of cats – people can be very... unkind," Huw says, as he tickles me under my chin and gives me a quick rub behind the ears.

"A very wise choice," I miaow-purr at him, and I am sure he understands. Cat-lovers like Huw always do.

I do my tricks for Huw too – my question mark tail, my crossed and uncrossed paws, my ear waggling thing – and he smiles and laughs so much. I love making him happy.

Huw is a poet and a painter. He spends his days making paintings which he then takes away to sell in the nearby town. That is when he is not on his computer doing digital paintings and other things, or chatting to other humans online.

I have no idea if the paintings are any good, or the poetry – it's more of a two-legs thing. We cats don't really do art and poetry.

Maybe that is because we *are* art and poetry!

Huw always comes back happy from town, but smells bad – because of what he has been drinking.

Then, often, he spends days drinking from the bottles of wine and beer and stronger stuff he has brought home from shopping.

He does not do very much then, just listens to music and sings along, and does not seem to eat much either – though he never forgets to feed me or give me fresh water.

I also have an automatic biscuit feeder and water fountain, so can survive here for many days alone. I have to do this when Huw gets so ill he has to go into hospital.

Sometimes, his sister Helen comes round. She has a kind round face and always tickles my tummy and gives me treats, which I like. She does the cleaning and also goes shopping for Huw when he is recovering from illness.

I can see the sadness in Huw's eyes when he is like this, and comfort him, cuddling up close and purring, as is my duty as a courteous, loyal and honourable cat.

I have seen this darkness in humans before, and sometimes in cats too.

"The meaning of life is that it ends, Merlin," he sighs sadly, kissing the top of my head. "Live all the days of your life...and I shall too..."

Every few weeks or so, we drive off in the camper van and stay in all sorts of places, sometimes nearby and sometimes very far away – and occasionally over the sea. This is great fun, I must say – I like travelling and trying foreign food.

Once, we go back to Spain, but never to plastic land, thank goodness. Helen comes with us sometimes. Huw never drinks too much when we go away though.

We live like this for several years, with Huw working on painting and poetry when he is well, then drinking a lot when he is not, which makes things worse – always.

Helen helps us get by when Huw is not well, and I am here to cheer him up.

We grow old together over the years, as I feel myself getting slower. I sleep more hours a day now, my backbone aches and my paws are stiff.

And then, one day, Huw seems very sick indeed.

But I am ill too, because I am not as young as I was either...

We lie on the bed, listening to the rain drizzling down outside for hours.

Then, eventually, later that night, we pass away together in each other's arms.

As my breathing stops, I think I can see colourful swirls like strands of smoke dancing around each other up in the sky.

But my task is not yet done.

I have more to do.

I have to find Sami, so I return to earth.

CHAPTER EIGHTEEN

In my sixth life, I enter showbusiness.

I am a circus cat in a big country called the USA.

We travel around all over, driving for miles and miles, putting up our big circus tent in towns big and small.

It is such great fun!

My name here is Minette and I am, of course, the star of the show.

I am the most beautiful 'calico' she-cat, with tortoiseshell and white fur. My chest and front paws are snowy-white, with orange and black patches all over my back and sides and face.

They say I have the most gorgeous green eyes too – just like Sami. I have not forgotten her and never will. It is my duty to find her and I shall – one day.

My new humans are LeShawn and Shantel, a couple who feed me well – and I look after them too.

"Where you at, cat?" says LeShawn when he is looking for me.

Then I dash to him from out of nowhere and leap up into his arms, as if I'm on springs! That makes him laugh, though his wife Shantel tends to roll her eyes at such fun and games.

"Clever girl!" LeShawn always says. "You got it! You a smart cat, Minette."

And I miaow and chirrup back in agreement as I head-bonk his face.

They are both circus performers – LeShawn is a magician and Shantel his assistant, and a dancer too.

The circus is full of people from so many different countries. They have all different skin colours, from dark black right the way through to the whitest white with some of the blonde dancing girls, and an albino African acrobat couple.

LeShawn and Shantel are both black, but not as dark-skinned as Yumi – I hope he is doing well with his family back home in Africa.

The circus performers are of different heights too. The tallest two-legs is the tallest human I have ever seen – *ever!* And he is even taller when he gets up on stilts.

Then there are the little people – 'dwarfs' as LeShawn calls them before Shantel tuts and tells him off for using the word. Some of them are great acrobats and others are clowns. I like them all.

All except one...

Kenny the clown is such a show-off he never wants to leave the stage and even goes out in front of the audience interrupting other performers' acts if we let him. So the ringmaster gets other performers to stop him – and also asks me to watch him backstage and yowl if he tries to run on stage.

Kenny has so many stars in his eyes that he is blind to his bad attention-seeking behaviour. It is like an illness really, this insatiable hunger for fame and attention – like a disease deep in the soul.

He resents me guarding him backstage, though, and has pulled my tail out of spite on occasion.

That is just *so* mean!

There are many different two-legs languages spoken at the circus.

We have acrobats from China and other parts of Asia, magicians from Arabia and Africa, tightrope walkers from France and Germany, trapeze artists from Spain and Italy and all over.

The ringmaster is a big fat man called Sasha, from Russia, and his assistant and best friend Vladimir is one of the clowns.

There are no animals in the circus apart from me and some little dogs. I like them as far as it goes, though I always allow for the limitations of their primitive species – as I do with humans too, of course. Such politeness and good manners befit the best mannered of courteous cats.

They are always there, the little white dogs, their pink tongues hanging out and their little tails waggling in the most doolally fashion!

In the circus, I get dressed up in a costume – which I would not usually approve of in cats, but as I have been doing this from when I was a tiny little kitten, it is fine. Often it is a smart red ringmaster suit costume, though I have others – sparkly dresses with sequins, a harlequin outfit, a beefeater suit and a lion costume complete with mane, and many, *many* more.

Then I go out in front of all those people and miaow and yowl orders to the little dancing dogs, who then jump through hoops and rings held up by LeShawn or Shantel or other performers. It is *so* funny!

At the end of my performance, I chase the little dogs out of the ring.

Both the big and little two-legs in the audience laugh so much at the sight, and clap and cheer. They are not used to cats chasing dogs – though it happens more than most people realise, I can tell you.

I also help in other acts, such as when I hold on to the shoulders of trapeze artists as they swing in the air, high above the ground, and with no safety net. They are very brave – as, of course, am I.

I sometimes assist LeShawn with his magic act, appearing in a puff of smoke when he waves his wand. It's a secret trick, so I cannot tell you exactly how we do it, or how we do the mind reading. But it is *very* impressive and the audience love it!

One day, we are performing somewhere in Middle America. I am not sure where precisely because everything also looks the same in these places – endless shopping malls everywhere. It's a good job Sasha the ringmaster is the one doing the talking and welcoming the audience at every performance – he always mentions the town we are in.

So I am there, in my smart red ringmaster costume, warming up for my performance with the acrobats, jugglers, clowns and trapeze artists, making sure Kenny the clown does not run out into the ring and spoil everything.

The tightrope walker is out there now with his act high up in the air, doing all sorts of tricks – standing on one leg, jumping up and down, lying down on his back. The spectators gasp and cheer.

And then I smell it.

That familiar smell:

Shaheen!

But more than that.

I smell a smell I have been waiting to smell for many years – in five new lives:

Sami!

We cats never forget a smell – of another cat or a two-legs. And we are *never* ever wrong – not when it comes to the nose department.

Sami is here!

Tonight!

I am *so* excited I run out to the side of the circle, sniffing the location of her smell. My insides are made of butterflies!

And then I see her. Towards the back of the audience, next to the aisle.

She is no longer a child, of course. It is many years since I saw her. I have absolutely no idea how and why she is in America.

Sami is all grown up now, a beautiful young woman – and oh so pretty! Next to her is an older lady with grey hair – her mum, Miriam. And there are two small two-legs with them – little children – one boy and one girl.

Standing beside them is Shaheen, though they clearly cannot see him – only I can. He looks at me and smiles. Then he runs up and down the steps laughing and giggling, with his red cape flapping behind him playing superheroes again.

I miaow with joy, then yowl loudly in Sami's direction – but I can tell she does not hear me past the noise of the circus and the audience.

But then someone calls my name:

"Minette! You on now, girl!"

It is LeShawn.

"Where you at, cat?"

I look at the circus ring and Kenny the show-off clown is on when he isn't supposed to be again – Sasha and Vladimir will tell me off later for that. I should have been guarding him.

I sigh sadly. I badly want to run up to where Sami is – hug her, kiss her, do my tricks for her and head bonk her so hard as I purr the loudest purr I have ever purred!

But I have a duty to perform.

A cat duty – which is the biggest duty of all.

I was born into the circus, and it has been good to me.

I cannot let them all down now.

As they say, the show must go on.

Sami and her mum are in the audience and are not going anywhere.

So I shall do my performance with the little dogs.

Then, after the show, I shall run up the steps to Sami and hug her harder than I have hugged anyone ever before!

And we shall be together again for ever and ever and ever!

CHAPTER NINETEEN

The audience love the act, as always.

LeShawn is brilliant – his magic amazes everyone who sees it.

I appear and disappear in a puff of smoke, as does Shantel, and all the people clap and cheer.

I wonder why Sami and her mum do not recognise me in the circus act, but then I remember that I am no longer ginger and white, as I was when I knew Sami in my first life. Now I look totally different, a calico cat, black and orange and white.

But then I do use my counting trick as part of the mind-reading act. If Sami sees that, surely she will know it's me?

This is the last trick I do – the end of LeShawn's act. Jugglers and clowns run on as we leave the ring.

I immediately look up to where Sami is sitting.

But the seats where she and her mum and the two small two-legs were sitting are now empty.

Noooooo!

My heart sinks.

I have to find Sami!

She must have left early for some reason, and that means she will probably be out in the parking lot.

I dash to the back door but then –

YANK!

Someone grabs my tail and pulls me back.

I protest loudly with yowls, then turn to see who it is.

Kenny the clown – and with such a snide smile smeared on his face.

I beg him to let me go, but he doesn't. Instead, he shuts me inside a cage, one of the ones used for the little dogs.

"That'll teach you, fleabag!" he laughs nastily, leaving me there alone.

I plead with him to let me out:

Miaow-miaow-miaow-yow-yow-yowl!

But it is no good, and everyone else is too busy to notice that I am trapped.

Later – much later – LeShawn finds me and lets me out of the cage.

"Wassup, Minette?" he asks as he lifts me up.

But I am too depressed to do anything but utter a low yowl. I know it is too late – Sami will be long gone, and I have no way of finding her again.

"You gotten sick on me, girl?" he says, frowning.

I bury my face in his neck and wail.

Then I growl as I see Kenny the clown stroll by smiling smugly.

But the show must go on – though I seem to have lost all my energy, and have no enthusiasm for anything.

We travel on highways and freeways to town after town, but it's all such a blur to me these days – there is no longer a spring in the step of my paws, and all my miaows are quiet and weak.

LeShawn and Shantel call the vet. As ever, I am poked and prodded in all sorts of sensitive places, but they can find nothing wrong.

Then Sasha and Vladimir come to see me.

"I am *fink* maybe cat is depressed," announces Sasha the ringmaster.

"Me also," says Vladimir, his sad Slavic eyes peering deeply into mine.

"Depressed?" says LeShawn, shaking his head. "Man, that cat live the life – how come he depressed? It me who should be depressed and ain't that the truth, what with..."

He sees Shantel standing nearby with her hands on her hips staring at him, and does not finish the sentence.

And so, the vet gives me a couple of shots – vitamins, apparently – and then we are back on the road again.

LeShawn is with me in the back of the trailer. He watches me staring out of the window at the fields and trees by the freeway as we are driven to our next destination.

"You looking for someone, girl?" asks LeShawn and I hop up and miaow a loud 'YES' that even the dimmest of two-legs could understand.

"Great big *yuge* world out there, Minette, and ain't that the truth?" he says. "But how can I help you if I don't know who you lookin' for?"

This is the problem with human-cat communication – it does have its limits.

I know LeShawn would help if he could, but I am not able to tell him about Sami or what she looks like – or where she lives – because I do not know either.

I curl up in a ball and try to sleep.

I hope I dream of Sami. I usually do.

Then, it is show time again.

And I am so tired.

Tired of the circus.

Tired of the nasty show-off Kenny the clown taunting me and pulling my tail.

Tired of it all – everything and everyone.

I probably should not have gone out that night to perform.

But we cats have a duty and refuse to let others down. Besides, we hide our feelings always, especially if we are not feeling well. This helps us survive, but it does have its downside.

That night I am due to be part of the trapeze act.

I am about to go on when Kenny the clown yanks my tail.

Right!

THAT IS IT!

I have had *enough.*

The *rule of law* is all very well...

But now it is time for:

The rule of claw!

I can do touchy-feely, yes – but I also do *scratchy-bleedy* when pushed!

I turn round and scram Kenny on his smug grinning face with a loud catty hiss.

SCRAAAAAMMMMM!

HSSSSSSSSS!

Everyone backstage is shocked. I have never scrammed anyone before –

Never ever **EVER!**

However, I know a lot of people are sick of Kenny the clown's behaviour, so some even start applauding what I have done.

Kenny's face darkens to an ugly shade of anger, and a colour I have not seen before. And then he gives me a massive kick with his big clown shoes. Just once – but once is enough.

I feel a sudden sharp pain inside.

Like something in there is broken – damaged – hurt. I can feel it.

"That is *it!*" I hear Sasha yell to Kenny backstage. "You are *out*! You leave! You go now!"

And then I am on – out in front of the audience.

The show must go on...

Soon I am on the shoulder of an acrobat called Francisco swinging high on the trapeze.

Then in mid-air I hop onto the shoulder of his wife Juliana, who is a very slightly-built female two-legs.

This is usually fun. But it is not fun tonight.

I feel really ill now, aching inside – and weak.

I only just manage to hop onto Juliana's shoulder.

My hold is not as secure and stable as it usually is, and I am not well balanced at all.

Balance is *everything* when you are high up in the air. Ask a tweety bird next time you meet one.

I can sense Juliana becoming tense, as she swings in mid-air.

I look down at the ground – no safety net in this circus.

The fact is I am wobbly on Juliana's shoulders and that is making her lose her grip of the bar on the trapeze.

The audience gasps as she lets go with one hand.

So she is now holding on with the fingers of the other – just one hand grip separates her from certain death on the ground below. This is very dangerous indeed.

My wobbly weight on her shoulder is making her unbalanced.

She will fall if I do not do something – if I do not act –

If I do not let go.

And so I let go...

And I plummet down to the ground below.

Down, down, down to my doom – though I know Juliana will live on because of my sacrifice.

It is, perhaps, the best way for a circus cat to go.

CHAPTER TWENTY

My new mum makes lovely tasty milk and has a pretty pink tongue to lick and wash us with.

She is very young, and we are her first kittens – me and my brothers and sisters – and what a kerfuffle of kittens we are!

I have been born a feral tom kitten living in the ruins of Rome in Italy.

I am mostly black, but with some brown patches on my face and body.

Being a feral cat, with no human, I have no name – though my mum has a special name for me. One which no two-legs could possibly understand.

I love her so much – her fluffy black fur, her warm hugs and the way she helps me up to her tummy to get my feed of delicious milk, so I can grow big and strong.

She knows I find it hard to breathe and have done since I was born. I wheeze and cough a lot, and sometimes feel very weak. I do not know why.

Lots and lots of cats and kittens live here in the ancient ruins. There are so many hiding places – and we all hide away and sleep during the hot days when the tourists are milling and mooching around taking photos.

We only come out when it's cooler, especially at night, which is when the mice come out to play too. *What luck!*

My mum is a great hunter and brings back lots of them for us all to eat when our kitten teeth are strong enough for solids.

There is also a lot of uneaten food and rubbish thrown away by tourists – which can be rather tasty too.

We may just be feral cats without a human home, but kind people come and feed us sometimes, and vets give us check-ups too.

This is when they lift me up and listen to my chest.

My mum looks on with a worried expression on her little whiskery face. I am her smallest kitten and not yet old enough to go it alone, so she protects me – always.

She knows these people mean no harm, so just watches patiently as they examine me. Then one of them gives me an injection. It's a little bit hurty, but not *too* much. They say I have been a very brave little kitten and put me back with my mum, who licks me all over to give me her smell again.

My brothers are sisters are bigger than me, and none of them wheeze and cough as I do.

That is why I stay close to my mum, cuddling up to her when the other kittens have gone out exploring. It is always so warm and safe with her. I love my mum so much!

She licks and kisses me, and teaches me to wash myself as well, and in the right order:

Paws, face, ears, chest, back, tail, tummy, bottom.

I am so lucky to have her, to be alive in this place at this time.

Sometimes, my mum sings to me as I fall asleep – old cat songs as ancient as the ruins in which we live.

And sometimes my mum tells me about my ancestors, who lived here many lifetimes ago, with the Roman emperors and their great armies, in a big bustling city where anything and everything was possible.

We live near the Colosseum. My mum tells me about the massive colossal statue of the emperor Nero which used to stand nearby and gave the big amphitheatre its present name.

She tells me about all the chariot races and gladiators fighting to the death, and how they even had events with wild exotic animals like lions and tigers, leopards and elephants, and even hippos and crocodiles when they filled the arena full of water for the spectacular shows.

She talks of the great emperors – Julius Caesar, Augustus, Hadrian, Claudius – and how their empire ruled the known world.

How peoples from all over that empire – both free people and slaves – came to Rome from other places in Europe, and even Africa and Asia, like the wild animals.

How all the goods and products and treasures from the four corners of the earth ended up in Rome – from the finest jewels and precious stones like diamonds, sapphires, rubies and emeralds, fine cloth and silk from the east, ivory and animal skins from Africa, gold and tin from Britain, including lead from Cornwall for the pipes and plumbing.

Rome truly was the centre of the world and its largest city, with a million people – and not a few cats!

And my mum says it was my cat ancestors who were there – witnessing it all, catching mice in the grain stores and on the ships that built an empire, in the streets and houses of the city, as the citizens of Rome hustled and bustled on the busy streets, all those centuries ago.

The greatness of Rome would not have been possible without cats – they would have been overrun with vermin in weeks without us.

The same goes for all great civilisations.

Cats truly are the kings of the world!

I am so proud of this that my little kitten heart swells at the thought of it.

But I know I am not well.

I have never been all that well.

I was born wrong inside – my heart and lungs are not as they should be.

I know that, and always have, as has my dear mum.

I do my best though, and do not give in. Every breath is a blessing in life.

But I always knew the day would come when my weak heart and lungs could no longer keep me alive, when my wheezing and coughing would become too bad to bear.

And that day is today.

I am too weak to even stand up on my own now and am in a lot of pain.

When the humans who check on us cats come, both they and I know that it is time. So does my lovely mum, who gives me a final big hug and kiss and head-bonk.

It is time to say goodbye.

But I am not sad, because as my mum always says:

Don't wail because it's over – miaow because it happened!

We touch noses and chirrup a loving farewell with a final purr.

Then, a human hand strokes my head and I feel the tiniest prick of a needle in my neck.

And so I drift away into a beautiful painless sleepy dream, looking at the loving face of my lovely mum as my little kitten life fades away forever.

CHAPTER TWENTY-ONE

Red and yellow and orange flower petals are scattered everywhere, floating and fluttering down like confetti, or leaves from autumn trees, or a million tiny butterflies.

Noisy drums, cymbals, tambourines and bells sound loudly in the streets.

Jingle-Jangle, Jingle-Jangle!

What a racket!

A symphony of smells is twitching in my nostrils – so many different food smells and perfumes and spices, odours and scents of every imaginable kind.

There are crowds of people parading and dancing along in the festival, smiling and singing and praying – to *me.*

Because in this, my eighth life is in India, I am a god.

Or, more specifically, a goddess.

Or, actually, even more specifically, I am the cat called Vahana who carries the mother goddess Shashti – the protector of children – on my back.

According to legend anyway...

Though I carry no-one on my back now, but I play the role well.

The goddess Shashti is actually only a colourfully painted wooden statue being held aloft on another float, not a real two-legs being that breathes. But the statue represents the goddess and all she stands for. It is an honour to serve her.

We have our own temple, where I live in the style to which I have been accustomed – since birth. I want for nothing and only eat the finest food, and plenty of it, as befits such a noble cat of high birth.

Only the best for me!

The statue of Shashti is usually kept at the centre of the temple, and this is where people leave offerings and gifts.

In this life, I am a beautiful blue Persian cat, with well-groomed long silvery fluffy fur, a round sweet face and the most beautiful blue eyes which shine bright like the bluest sapphires, day and night.

I am being carried aloft on a platform, with garlands of colourful red and yellow and orange flowers draped and festooned everywhere.

All the humans young and old bow to me as I pass by. I acknowledge their worship and praise with a little sniff of my pretty pug-nose, an occasional twitch of a whisker, and a casual wave of my fluffy superior paw.

Sometimes I may blink approval too, or give a little chirrup of thanks – though a silent miaow is more usual. I don't want to overdo it!

Some of the two-legs give offerings – money and jewellery, neither of which interest me. Or food, which always does.

I do not eat the very sweet or the hottest spicy food offered though, or any of the fruit. That fare is only fit for humans!

I am, however, rather partial to any of the meat and fish dishes the worshippers of Shashti wish to give.

And as my goddess cannot eat anything herself on account of her being statue made of wood, so not even alive at all, I have the pick of the feast – which means all the more for me!

Hoorah!

As a consequence, I am rather well-padded, it's true – though I see absolutely nothing to be ashamed of in my wondrous plumpity.

It is just how I am in this life. And besides, I do not have to run very fast, or hunt anything, because everything is done for me.

The humans would probably wash me too if I asked them – but there are limits.

I know I live a privileged and lucky life – far luckier than many of the two-legs who come to the festival or visit my temple home. Some of them are very poor indeed, and pray to the goddess to protect their children and wish them health and wealth in life.

All money donated to the temple goes to helping the poor, especially the children, and the staff cook hot meals for free every day for anyone who needs feeding.

There are a lot of festivals with noise and crowds and smells and flowers all the time, so I am well used to it. I play my role magnificently, I must say, and everyone loves me and is so happy to have met the cat called Vahana who, according to legend, was so dear to the mother goddess Shashti.

And then I smell it.

A smell I have smelt so many times before in my previous lives:

Shaheen!

I look around frantically, pinpointing the exact scent location with little sniffs of my pretty pug-nose.

And then I see him.

There, in the crowd, with his red coat flapping like a superhero cape behind him, laughing and giggling in the middle of the festival.

He looks right at me and smiles.

And I know that my dream is not over.

I know there is a chance I may see Sami again, and have faith that I will.

How, I do not know – especially as I came so close at the circus in the USA but lost her.

Is she still even there? How was she there in the first place? And how on earth can I find her – wherever she is now?

I have no idea.

But somehow, I believe all things are possible.

That is what Shaheen is telling me, with his smile.

A warm wave of self-belief washes over me and I know everything will be alright.

We all need faith in ourselves, to believe that we can do it.

Shaheen has given me mine, and I am so glad he has been there in my many lives, making me remember and giving me confidence in myself to achieve my goal – to be reunited with Sami once again.

That night, back at the temple, after enjoying so much of the really delicious dinner I have been given that I can hardly walk, I settle down to sleep.

Being a noble cat living in a temple, I always sleep on cushions made of the finest fabric and silk, in a little space behind a curtain not far from the statue of Shashti. We are surrounded by golden ornaments and garlands of beautifully scented flowers.

Outside, the moon is full and an owl *too-wit-too-woos* outside, amidst the crickets chirruping.

I feel so at home here, and am so very full of food. I burp a couple of times, then give myself a wonderful wash – and then, when I am ready, and am sure I have found the *purr-fect* place, I curl up comfy and prepare to drift off to sleep.

But in the middle of the night, my ears twitch me awake.

I hear a noise.

Footsteps. Hushed human voices.

And a very bad two-legs smell.

There are people in the temple!

People who should not be here.

People who have broken in.

Intruders!

CHAPTER TWENTY-TWO

Shhh!

Listen!

Someone is here!

Here – in the temple!

I stay as still and silent as I can, hiding behind my curtain on my cushions in the dark.

I am quiet as a mouse – as a cat – which takes some doing, I can tell you.

I try not to breathe, in case the intruders hear me.

But I have to breathe, of course, to stay alive – though I try to do so in a slow, low, non-sniffling manner. Which is quite a challenge with my snuffly little Persian pug nose, purr-fect though it is.

I see electric torchlight through the curtain into the darkness and hear whispers.

Then I hear items being taken from shelves, and humid little human hands opening drawers and searching the inside of the main temple for valuables.

Thieves.

I knew it!

The stinky stench of the worst of two-legs enters my nostrils.

Yeeeuuuccckkk!

It really pongs!

The smell is nasty and rotten and, well, just plain nasty.

I am really not used to horrible smells.

I am a noble holy cat and live like a princess in sweet-smelling luxury.

So I am used to the best of scents and smells – such as delicious foods or the most lovely of perfumes.

And the thing is – and I know this from experience – horrible smells make me sneeze something terrible.

So then I feel it, in my pretty little pug nose – the first itch of a sneeze.

It grows and grows, like a small flame becoming a raging forest fire.

Until, eventually, I can no longer hold it in, or swallow it down, or wish it away.

And then:

AAAAACCCCCHHHHHOOOOOOOOOO!

Whoops!

The sneeze is perhaps the loudest sneeze I have ever sneezed in my life!

Suddenly, the curtain is yanked back.

And a bright blinding torchlight beam is shone in my face.

A gust of yucky thief smell hits me.

And I growl a low growl of catty grump growl at being so rudely disturbed.

When my eyes get used to the light, I see before me an ugly old witch with a thin pointed chin and an eye patch.

She grins nastily to show the few broken black and yellow rotten teeth that remain in her skull.

Her breath stinks of the worst stinky-stink ever!

I breathe through my mouth, so as to try not to smell it, but it is too late and – I sneeze, again, right in her face:

AAAAACCCCCHHHHHOOOOOOOOOO!

The mean old crone sneers something, and from the tone of her voice I know this human is a cat-hater. I can tell immediately from the stinky hateful smell.

The witch hisses a whisper at the other thieves, and two men appear.

One young and short, no more than a boy, who looks worried and nervous.

The other is as ugly as the old witch woman – a very fat man, with a greasy black beard and one big gold earring. He is holding a sack jangling with what I presume to be the gold and silver goblets and statues, and other ornaments and valuables, he has taken from the temple shelves.

"Kill it," snaps the fat man, coldly.

I glare back at them and hiss.

The boy looks worried and sad – I can smell that he is no cat hater and does not want me to be hurt.

"B-b-but it is b-b-better if we are finding all the m-m-money first, no?" says the boy.

Silence.

Then the old witch speaks.

"He's right. You find the money. I'll watch the thing."

The thing?

The thing?

THE THING?!!!

I am a noble high-born cat, the present incarnation of Vahana who carried the mother goddess Shashti – the protector of children – on her back.

What I am most definitely not is a 'thing'!

I give the mean old witch a very hard stare indeed.

Then I yowl a yowl so loud, screech a screech so piercing, and hiss a hiss so hissy, that the noise will surely be heard by any animal for miles around.

YOWWWLLLMIIIAAAOOOWWWAAARRRGGGHHHSSSSS!!!

Just like that.

"Shut it up!" yells the man who is shining his torch in the darkness, trying to find where the bank notes, coins and jewellery donated to the temple are stashed – the funds we use to feed the poor and desperate.

At that, I miaow a miaow so loud that even some of the two-legs species somewhere must have heard me – though their ears, as we all know, are primitive indeed and do not seem to hear very much at all most of the time.

Then the old crone lunges forward and grabs me – in a rather sensitive place too, I must say.

And, with something of a struggle, she picks me up and holds me firm against her chest, trying to put her hand over my miaowing, yowling, growling mouth which is making the most awful noises I think it has ever made.

"Shut up shut up shut up!" hisses the witch.

But I don't, of course. Instead, I twist and wriggle like a big furry worm in her old bony hands.

"M-m-maybe b-b-be n-n-nice to her...I m-m-mean, stroke her to c-c-calm her down?" says the nervous-looking boy.

I catch his eye. A cat-lover – I can always tell. I can also see, and smell, the sadness in him.

Then, somehow, I am upside down in the mean old witch's arms, with my bottom pushed right in her face.

It is too good an opportunity to miss!

And so, with an enormous push, I do the biggest, most smelly smell of a fart right into her ugly one-eyed face – and nose.

I have eaten plenty of spicy meat at the festival, so my smells are at peak stink – but this smell is perhaps the worst smell my bottom has ever burped!

Immediately, the old crone lets go and I run and hide behind the goddess statue.

Just then, the door is smashed down and the temple staff turn on the lights. They are with the police, who then grab the thieves, catching them red-handed, before taking them away.

"That damn cat!" spits the fat man as he is handcuffed.

"Hssssss!" spits the witch woman at me as she leaves.

"I-I-I am sorry," says the boy, and I miaow back and bow my thanks to him.

The temple staff see this, and go with him and the police – I hope he does not get into too much trouble.

I am, of course, praised by all and sundry for being the hero I am, saving precious statues and ornaments at the temple, and preventing the money donated to help the poor from being stolen by the greedy thieves – who, it turns out, are part of a gang that has been stealing from many temples here for years.

A great many precious artefacts from other temples have been retrieved and returned to their rightful homes since the gang was caught and their hide-out raided.

I am even awarded a bright shiny silver medal for bravery by the police – with a wonderful purple ribbon too.

Purple for a princess, I always say!

Best of all, the boy who stopped the thieves killing me was spared prison and, to make up for his part in the thefts, has become a monk at my temple. He is now the one who cares for me, feeds me and grooms my beautiful blue Persian fur every day.

It turns out he was kidnapped when he was a small child by the criminal gang and taken away from his real family.

He has chosen a new name for himself too for his new temple life – Rahmat, which means 'mercy'.

And so we live here happily, helping the poor and needy, feeding the hungry and taking part in the many festivals – which is always great fun.

However, all things must pass, and eventually my old heart gives out – at least partly a result, it has to be said, of my well-padded plumpity and all the delicious dishes I have so enjoyed eating, perhaps a little too much.

And so endeth my eighth life.

CHAPTER TWENTY-THREE

The world is white – again.

But this time I watch the falling snow from the warmth of a cosy living room.

My name is Bella and my two-legs is a lovely old lady called Marjorie.

I am a beautiful black and white cat again – a tuxedo cat, which means I have a black coat with a white bib on my chest.

My face is ever so sweet and pretty, with the white fur extending over my mouth and jaw, and then continuing up past my pretty pink nose, which has long white whiskers either side, and onto my forehead.

I walk about on four wonderful white paws at the end of my black legs, and I boast a black tail with a tip of pure white, like a magician's wand. *Magic!*

My two-legs calls me affectionate and playful, and very intelligent too – which, as a cat, I already know of course, but it doesn't hurt being reminded from time to time.

My eyes are bright and yellow and see everything, often from the window of the house in winter, though I do also go out on my daily patrols in the snow to check all is well.

However, I am *really* glad I do not live outside. Here in Canada, it is freezy cold at this time of year!

Marjorie is very old. She has been adopted by several cats in the past – photographs of them in silver frames sit on shelves and windowsills around the house. These cat cousins are all long gone over the rainbow bridge, of course. I nod to them whenever I walk by, as a sign of respect for all those who came before me.

I purr a lot here. I like purring, and Marjorie feeds me the most delicious food every day, and gives me plenty of cuddles too, so I purr even more.

Most evenings I spend lying on her lap purring myself to sleep while she watches TV, or listens to the radio and reads.

It is a delightful feline life – I have fallen on all four paws again!

Until, one day, it all changes.

Because my lovely two-legs lady, who I have looked after and loved all my life, passes away. I find Marjorie one day, sitting in her armchair, absolutely still but not asleep. And I know immediately that she, too, has gone over the rainbow bridge.

What to do?

Well, what can I do?

There is food and water aplenty here for me, and an automatic feeder and water fountain.

I shall just have to wait for Marjorie's friends to come round, as they often do. They will then raise the alarm when she does not respond.

I have no idea, however, what will become of me.

And so, the phone rings and rings. Then, a while later, the doorbell rings too and there are loud knocks – and then someone turns a key in the lock and comes in.

I know the smell – it is Marjorie's old friend, Edith.

She finds Marjorie in her armchair and sighs, though she does not seem shocked. No doubt she has seen many an old friend pass away after a long life.

"Poor puss," she says to me, and I miaow mournfully back. "I wish I could take you home, little girl, but they won't allow it in my sheltered housing."

I chirrup a *'never mind, I understand'* in her direction.

"Besides, you wouldn't want to be cooped up in an apartment never going out, would you?"

We look out together at the snow blanketing the garden and leafless trees.

"Anyhoo, Justin and Sophie will know what to do."

I wince and cringe, and very nearly cough up a furball.

Justin is Marjorie's son – and I know from his occasional visits how much he hates cats. Sophie is her daughter and visits only at Christmas, and then only sometimes as she works in the big busy city in her big busy career.

But, what will be, will be.

Edith checks on my food and water, and empties my litter tray, I thank her with a miaow and a nod of gratitude. Not every two-legs is as considerate, I know.

"We gotta do something 'bout that damn animal, eh?" yells Justin, who is overweight, bearded and wearing his usual builder's work overalls.

After the funeral director takes Marjorie's body away, Justin immediately starts clearing the house, taking things to sell, including the silver photo frames. He rips out all the photos of cats and throws them in the bin.

Later today, they are coming to take away everything else – all the furniture etc.

A large '*FOR SALE*' sign is already standing on a post outside in the front garden.

Justin continues yelling into his mobile phone.

"Yeah, but you can't have a cat in your Toronto apartment, you ain't never there, and I..."

He laughs nastily.

"I can't – y'know I hate cats. They stink – they're unhygienic, disgusting, full of fleas and disease..."

I hiss and growl at his insults, from where I am hiding bravely under the dining table.

"And this one's mostly black, so hard to rehome they say, and it isn't even declawed – who's gonna wanna to pay for that, eh? The shelter puts down strays all the time – I already called 'em."

Well, that was it!

I'd had *quite* enough!

We cats may play the innocent, but trust me, we *always* know what's going on.

You think we can't understand you?

You humans, you two-legs, you creatures of just about the most primitive species known to cat?

Well, *think again!*

We do – everything you say, and in any language, all the time.

We can smell the words, the feelings, the good – or bad – intentions.

We can sense the pain, the joy, the love and the hate.

That is why we make such wonderful and loving pets.

It is also why we are the world's greatest survivors – and escape artists.

I choose my next move *most* carefully.

I wait until I hear the removals van arrive and come to a halt in the drive.

Then, I pad so softly and quietly behind Justin's back with my little white paws that he does not hear me at all.

So, when he opens the front door –

WHOOSH!

– I am out. Swift as an arrow.

Gone!

Outside in the cold and snow.

"Hey!" yells Justin, the cat-hater.

But I do not stop.

I run and I run and I run, and do not look back until I am all alone, in a wood, and hiding behind a bush.

It is so cold that my breath makes smoke in the air and my ears are freezy cold.

I remember another life, lived amongst the snow and ice...

I have no idea really how to survive in this landscape, as I have always been a house cat, and very well fed too. I have never had to hunt or find my own food.

But, as my much-missed two-legs Marjorie always used to say with her lovely smile:

'Something will turn up!'

So I start walking, near – but not on – a main road, and wait for something to happen.

Because, as experience has taught me in my many lives, it usually does.

CHAPTER TWENTY-FOUR

"Good morning. I am Victor."

"Hello," I say, blinking up at him, "I'm...Summer."

Bella was my name with the dear departed Marjorie. It is not my name any more.

Inside, I am Summer.

Inside, I have always been Summer, and always will be.

After I run away, I follow the road for a couple of days, and am approaching a city called Ottawa when I first meet Victor.

I am so hungry that I'm rooting around in the big bins in an alley behind some restaurants and shops.

I jump up and balance on the rim of the bin, leaning in to reach a tasty morsel of food I have smelt in there somewhere.

And then –

CRRRRRAAAAASSSSSHHHHH!

– I fall in!

So I am lying there on my back on the pile of stinky garbage in the bottom of the bin, looking up at the starry sky.

It is a long way down.

Unfortunately, that means that it's an equally long way up!

I have no idea how I am going to get out of the big bin, so just lie there on my bed of trash and blink at the pretty, twinkly stars above, thinking about things...

Then, suddenly, a great big yellow eye is staring down at me from the sky.

It is huge!

A monster's eye!

But just one!

A one-eyed monster's eye!

But then I see a face looking down at me. It is a large handsome tabby tomcat face, with just one eye.

This is Victor.

"It is a world most dangerous out there, *mon petit chaton,"* he says, after he has helped me out, using the native French cat language from his home city of Montreal.

Victor is almost twice as big as me, with dark tabby colouring in his sleek fur. In a way, he looks a little scary, especially with his one big eye. But I soon learn he is perhaps the kindest, most considerate and polite cat I have ever met – and probably the most well-travelled too.

"Ah yes, I have been working as sailor cat, and have lived on many ships which are sailing all over the world, to the lands most strange..." he says, before telling me all about his exotic adventures overseas.

My tummy is so hungry, it rumbles.

"...and I was eating plenty of the fish most wonderful and colourful also."

Food – my favourite subject!

Victor can smell my hunger, so leads me to the secret places where we can find the best thrown-away food of all. He knows all the tricks.

That night, we eat very well, snug in a warm vent of an office block, safe away from all the snow.

"I was out at sea since many years, but then my ship, she sink, and so...*et voilà*...I am here."

I tell him my story, but only about this life, with my two-legs Marjorie – not the others.

"*Oh dommage,*" he says, "this is a shame. But the life, she continues, *non?*"

"*Non,*" I say, "I mean, yes! Life goes on. Always."

We fall asleep, well fed and firm friends, cuddling together to keep warm in our cubby hole tucked in an alley away from the street.

The smell of rain wakes me. Freezing rain.

It is early morning in Ottawa and the tweety birds are already busy singing.

Victor is not there.

I knew it was too good to be true – strays seldom stay in one place for long.

They *stray* – hence the name.

They do not stay.

If they did, they'd be called *'stays'*, not 'strays'...maybe...even though they're not.

You know what I mean...

"*Bonjour!*" announces Victor with a loud miaow, after he has dropped a dead rat at my feet. "Breakfast!"

I am *so* glad he has returned. I know I'd be pretty lost here on my own.

After eating, and having a good wash, we continue together on our way.

"Where are we going?" I ask Victor.

"Everywhere, and nowhere," he says. "We are free – free as the wind."

The wind is blowing bitter, even when the freezing rain stops, though we cats have thick fur which can and does keep out the cold.

The sub-zero temperatures mean we need more food to keep up our energy levels and stay warm inside, so this is always on our minds.

No litter bin or trashcan is safe from our curious noses. We sniff and explore every one we pass, and often find some tasty titbits in the waste too. The things people throw away!

That evening, I gorge myself on half a cold roast chicken that a supermarket has dumped in one of its huge bins – and they are so full of all sorts of other foods too.

But we are careful not to fall asleep in these big trash cans, even though they are cosy out of the wind. Big trucks collect them from time to time and take them away to the tip or an incinerator – and no cat wants to end up in either.

Take my advice – *never ever sleep in a bin!*

If you're a cat – or even if you aren't.

The next day, the weather is worse. The freezing rain lashes down, stinging my skin even under the fur.

"Keep on walking, Summer," miaow-shouts Victor through the whistling wind.

So I do.

I love the way Victor says my name, and squint a chirrup at him through the freezing rain. He seems to know where he's going anyway, and sings songs as we march along

– happy songs, and sea shanties, in his native language as well.

We are leaving the city – the houses and buildings become fewer and then end altogether as we enter the countryside.

Victor says he knows a warm place where food is plentiful – a food processing factory – and this is where we are heading. He says we can stay there safe for weeks until the weather gets better and the warmth thaws the ice and snow.

And then we come to a great big road. There is traffic on it, mostly trucks whizzing by, monstrous wheel-boxes with load roars and huge black wheels crushing the slush.

We walk along the road for some way, but there is no crossing or bridge anywhere.

The road cuts through the countryside, not a built-up area, so no human needs to cross it really, certainly not on foot.

We have to cross it, though – on paw.

But how?

Or, rather, where?

I then smell the smell I know so well, and see Shaheen on the other side of the highway, smiling and waving at me. I raise a paw to wave back and miaow hello.

"Who you are talking to?" asks Victor.

I say nothing.

He clearly cannot see Shaheen, but Victor also nods and sighs, which suggest he understands. I am clearly not the only cat to see such things.

I look through the freezing rain at the other side of the road again, but Shaheen has gone.

It is while we are sitting by the highway in silence, thinking how to cross it, that it happens.

There is a squeal of brakes and a truck skids and slides and jack-knifes.

The freezing rain has covered the tarmac in a layer of invisible black ice which is so slippery and dangerous.

The tanker has just delivered its petrol and is empty, so it has no weight to keep it pinned to the road...

I look straight at the truck's headlights as the great steel beast bears down on me, the bleep blaring in my ears.

Victor pushes me out of the way, but it is too late.

The world goes black, and I remember no more.

CHAPTER TWENTY-FIVE

I open my eyes.

The world is a great big blur, but slowly comes into focus, like water clearing in a muddy puddle after the rain.

I blink myself awake.

It is the smells that have woken me up.

I am in a place swirling with smells – animal scents of all sorts.

And that can only mean one thing:

I am at the vet's.

I have no memory of how I got here.

The last thing I remember is the freezing rain, the big road, a truck careering out of control – and Victor pushing me out of the way.

Where is Victor?

I cannot smell him, so I know he is not here with me, or anywhere near – our fabulously sensitive feline noses can detect cat scent at a great distance.

I sigh as I suspect the worst – another feline friend gone over the rainbow bridge too soon.

I am lying down in a cage, and notice I have some bandages on my body.

When I try to move, it hurts. I yowl low at the pain.

I feel very poorly – as weak as a kitten.

"Hello, cat," says a voice.

A young man two-legs peers into the cage at me. He smells kind.

"The vet'll be here later to check you over. You're a lucky girl, eh?"

I miaow back weakly. I just do not seem to have any energy to say or do more, and feel hurty in a lot of places.

And I feel tired – so very tired.

Exhausted.

Totally washed out.

Before I know it, I am yawning myself fast asleep again.

I wake later with a start.

That ***smell!***

I know ***that smell!***

But how can it be?

I try to stand but can't get up – I just do not have the strength.

Instead, I bend my neck to try and see who is there in the vet's surgery.

And then I see her:

Sami!

Sami, who was my first two-legs back in Syria.

Sami, who gave me my name – Summer.

Sami, who loved me so much and who I've been trying to find ever since, in all my lived lives.

She is in a white coat, as is the young man assistant.

Sami is a vet!

How brilliant is that?!!!

"The RTA cat's awake," says the assistant two-legs. "Seems to have survived OK. A real fighter."

"Another life gone, eh?" says Sami, with a different voice from the one I remember.

But now she is a much older two-legs – an adult. And her accent is a bit like the Americans I remember from the circus, which was the last time I saw and smelt her too – when she was up in the audience, watching the show...

I try to attract her attention, but am so weak I can hardly move.

I remember how Sami used to love my beautiful ginger and white fur coat, my little white paws and chest, and my twitchy tickly whiskers – and used to tell me so all the time.

But now I am black and white, and look totally different in this life.

So how on earth will Sami recognise me or know I am here at all?

"Let's have a look at her," says Sami, and the assistant opens my cage and lifts me onto the examining table.

Sami is so close to me now – I want to miaow loud so badly, but find I cannot make a sound.

Then Sami touches me.

Just the feel of her touching my fur makes my heart flutter like a furry butterfly.

I look up at Sami's face but it is blank – she does not recognise me at all. But then, why should she?

I lie there as she does the various tests, takes my temperature in a *very* intimate place indeed, looks into my eyes and mouth.

"She seems to be making good progress. I'll give her another shot of antibiotics, to stop any possible infection."

"Sami! Sami! It's me!" I try to wail, but nothing comes out of my open mouth.

Then I smell Shaheen and look up to see him standing there, smiling.

And suddenly, somehow, an energy enters me, and I feel strength growing inside, almost like a new life.

Sami used to love it when I twisted my tail into a 'question mark' shape, so I try to do it. But the effort is too great and my tail flops down limp by my side. No-one has seen me do it.

So I twitch one ear, then the other. I can do this more easily.

The young male two-legs sees this and walks over.

"Hey, look at this," he says. "Clever kitty!"

I smell Sami come closer too.

"That's odd," she says, frowning.

Then I manage to cross and uncross my paws, even with the bandages on.

"What is it?" asks the assistant.

"I...I don't know," says Sami. "Best give her the shot now."

And she does so, though I hardly feel the sharp little pain in my neck, I am so excited.

I keep crossing and uncrossing my paws, and waggling my ears.

"Never seen any cat do that before, eh?" says the young man.

"I have," whispers Sami, looking deep into my big green eyes. "I used to have an awesome clever cat, way back, in Syria, who did the exact same thing, but..."

I blink a 'hello' and she knows – I am *sure* she knows – it is me!

I am Summer – here again at last!

Here for you, Sami, here for you!

Here I am!

It's ME!

"Three," whispers Sami, holding up three fingers.

So I say:

"Miaow! Miaow! Miaow!"

Only small, weak miaows come out of my mouth, but they do come – and, more importantly, Sami hears them.

She gasps, a stunned expression on her face.

Then she holds up four fingers, so I say:

"Miaow! Miaow! Miaow! Miaow!"

Sami's mouth falls open in amazement.

"That's incredible," says the assistant. "She must be the cleverest cat in the whole world!"

"Summer?" mouths Sami, almost silently. "Is that *you?"*

"Yes yes YES! It's me – Summer!" I miaow, as loud as I can, my heart singing with joy. "And you are Sami, my two-legs Sami, my lovely Sami, and I am here again!"

Sami smiles warmly as she looks deep into my eyes, then headbonks her head gently against mine, the tears streaming down her face.

And then she gives me the biggest loving huggy hug I think anyone has ever had from anyone – ever!

CHAPTER TWENTY-SIX

With the arrival of spring, I am finally taken home with Sami.

Recovery has taken some time, but I am now almost all better, back standing on my own four paws, as befits a fit and healthy member of my noble species.

The biggest surprise of all is who is there to greet me.

I smell Honey as soon as I enter the house.

"Honey!" I miaow out loud.

We head bonk and touch noses – it's been a *long* time.

She is now, in this new life, the most beautiful torti-tabby cross she-cat. Her fur is lovely, the rich golden colour of runny honey.

"I can see you two are going to get along just fine," says Sami. "Summer, meet Honey."

Incredible!

Honey is called *Honey* here *too!*

Well, she has always been very sweet – but what are the chances, eh?

Honey is just what Sami happened to call her, and somehow she ended up here – before me.

Maybe it was all just meant to be?

Our cat destiny, as we live out our little lives here on earth.

"Mom, come and look," calls Sami.

Miriam shuffles into the room with her walking frame.

She is old and slow now, with white hair, and she cannot walk very well.

But this has not affected her smile, and she gives me a great big one.

"This is Summer," says Sami.

And she tells Miriam all about my tricks and how it's me, right here, reborn into this new life in Canada.

Her eyes moisten as she looks at a photograph on the windowsill.

"If only your father was here," she says.

"Yousuf died in London," Sami tells me – she is so sure now I can understand.

"He had a broken heart," whispers Miriam, "after Shaheen...left us...."

I miaow my condolences and rub against Miriam's legs to comfort her. She manages to lean down and gives me a quick rub behind the ears.

"But," she continues, "he got us out, legally, with the refugee resettlement program – that was so important for him."

Sami hugs her mum as they remember both Yousuf and Shaheen.

I am sitting admiring the comfy house when I hear the doorbell.

"That'll be David and the kids," says Sami.

A few moments later, two children rush into the room, a boy and a girl. They look the same age as Sami and Shaheen were when

I lived my first life with them in Syria, that war-torn land so far away.

"Aisha, Salam – this is Summer, our new cat."

And suddenly, I am picked up by Sami's daughter Aisha, who looks so like Sami when she was that age.

Salam is about the same age as Shaheen was when I knew him too, and seems a happy little boy. He strokes my fur gently.

I hope he does not pull my tail!

But I shall forgive him if he does...

Maybe...

So long as it's not *too* hard!

Then a man two-legs enters the room.

"Summer, meet David, my husband," Sami says to me.

I bow low in respect and miaow 'hello' at him.

"What a pretty kitty," he says, tickling me under my chin.

I like him!

And so, here I am, in my ninth and final life, reunited with Sami and her new family, and with the lovely Honey to keep me company too.

I feel so sad about Victor though – he gave his life saving mine.

But, as I am thinking this, I smell it – that proud tomcat smell – and I know.

"Victor!" I miaow loudly, and jump up onto the windowsill.

And there, out in the snow, and smiling wide with his one bright eye, is Victor, alive and well!

What a survivor!

WHAT A CAT!

He waves his big friendly paw at me, and I see him miaow a cheerful miaow of farewell through the glass.

I know Victor will never stop moving, never stop travelling to new places. Some cats are happy to live like that. It takes all sorts.

I wish him all the best and miaow my thanks at him as I wave my paw back to say a final goodbye to the most wonderful friend a cat could have.

How kind and polite of him to check I was alright before moving on. I shall never forget him.

Honey joins me on the windowsill as we watch Victor leave and melt into the landscape, padding through the snow like a panther, off into the bright fresh pine green of the springtime forest in the distance.

Sami picks me up in her loving arms and gives me a great big hug.

"I love you, Summer, I love you so much," she says, and I miaow back the exact same thing as I head bonk her beautiful face.

I look over her shoulder, staring out of the window at the wintery scene – and then I see him.

Shaheen!

He is standing there in the snow, smiling as always, his red coat hanging over his shoulders like a superhero cape.

Then Shaheen waves what I know will be a final wave of farewell – the last goodbye.

His job is done, his task complete.

As is mine, now I have fulfilled my purpose:

I am back with Sami at long last in my *furever* home.

I lift a paw to bid him farewell too.

Then he giggles and runs off into the distance, a true superhero, his red coat flapping behind him as his disappears into the misty distance – and is gone.

It is always hard to say goodbye, and so sad, but there is no other way.

We all experience both pain and joy on our journeys though life – and sometimes we find joy through pain too.

And it is amazing what we can all achieve if we have a dream.

All you need is a dream.

Then you can do it!

Yes, you can!

Just like I did.

We all have a place – a home – where we belong too.

And this is mine.

I am with Sami once again – and Honey, the loveliest cat in the whole wide world.

It has been difficult – but what is difficult is often good.

The struggle to achieve that final goal makes reaching it an experience all the more sweet.

As we cats always say:

Don't wail because it's over – miaow because it happened!

Life is good. A journey of hope and discovery.

For cats, all nine lives are good too, however they turn out.

And I have lived every one of my lives the best as I can.

There have been struggles and heartbreak, sorrow and pain.

But I am such a happy cat now that I am back with Sami.

And so, I snuggle up to her and Honey, safe in my *furever* home, as I purr myself into a deep sleepy dream.

Home at last.

The End

Printed in Great Britain
by Amazon